VOLCANO OF FIRE

Another You Say Which Way Adventure
by:

BLAIR POLLY & DM POTTER

ISBN-13: 978-1519197184
ISBN-10: 1519197187

How This Book Works

- This story depends on YOU.

- YOU say which way the story goes.

- What will YOU do?

At the end of each chapter, you get to make a decision. Turn to the page that matches your choice. **P62** means turn to page 62.

There are many paths to try. You can read them all over time. Right now, it's time to start the story. Good luck.

Oh … and watch out for the shape shifting plants!

VOLCANO OF FIRE

The Pillars of Haramon

You sit at a long table in the command pod atop one of the twin Pillars of Haramon. The room is filled with the hum of voices. A small robotic bird, unseen by those in the room, hovers in one corner.

The man at the head of the table has three blue-diamond stars pinned to his chest, indicating his rank as chief of the council. Next to him sits a visiting Lowland general, his face as hard as the rock walls of the command pod. Around the table, other important figures from both the Highlands and the Lowlands sit nervously.

Being the newest member of the Highland Council, you have yet to earn your first star, but you have big plans to make your mark.

"Quiet please," the chief says. "We've got important matters to discuss."

The chief's scars are visible, even from your seat at the opposite end of the table. These scars are proof of the many battles and expeditions he has taken part in over his long career and are proof of the dangers of living in the Highlands where the rock under your feet is the slipperiest material imaginable. Black glass.

"Supplies of tyranium crystals have run desperately

low," the chief says. "Without tyranium, workers can't move safely around the slopes and that means no progress on the trade routes being built between the Lowlands and the Highlands. If our truce is to last, trade is critical."

As you listen to the chief talk, you stare out of the large windows that overlook the slopes below. Further down Long Gully, the second pillar rises from the smooth black slope. A colony of red-beaked pangos squabble with each other for nesting spaces in the cracks near its summit.

To the south are the patchwork fields of the Lowlands, the blue ribbons of the river delta and the turquoise sea. Petron's smallest moon has just risen, pale pink in the morning light, just above the horizon.

"We need to mount an expedition to locate a new source of crystals, and soon," the chief says. "Led by someone we trust."

He turns and looks in your direction. "Someone who knows how to slide on black glass and has the ability to lead a team. Someone with a knowledge of mining and brave enough to take chances when necessary. Are you up for it?" the chief asks, catching you off guard.

"Me?" Sure you've been a troop leader in the Slider Corps and spent a little time in mining school, but leading an expedition into new territory? That's quite a responsibility.

The Lowland general stands, rests his hairy knuckles on the table before him, and leans towards your end of the table. "We need someone who is respected by both the Lowlanders and the Highlanders. Someone both sides trust to ensure an equal share of any discoveries."

"That's right," the chief says. "It was you who helped start the peace process. You are the logical choice."

Your part in this story is about to begin. You are being asked to undertake a dangerous mission, one that is important to your community. But are you really qualified? You are young. Surely others would be more suitable. Maybe you should suggest someone more experienced lead the expedition, then you could go back home and live a safe life growing hydro or hunting pangos.

It is time to make your first decision. Do you:

Agree to lead the mission? **P4**

Or

Suggest someone else lead the mission? **P11**

4

You have agreed to lead the mission.

"I'm happy enough to lead an expedition if I can choose the people I take with me," you say to the council.

"The Lowlands will need representation on this mission too," the Lowland general says. "I will send you six of my best troopers and you can choose which members of the Slider Corps and which miners to take. How does that sound?"

You look around the table at all the expectant faces, the chief's especially. "Okay," you say. "How soon do we leave?"

There is a look of relief on the chief's face. "As soon as we can gather the required personnel and equipment. The mission is to Mount Kakona."

"Mount Kakona?" you say, hoping you've misheard. "That's an active volcano, isn't it?"

The chief nods. "The biggest. But volcanoes are where the crystals are. Give me a list of the Highlanders you want to take along as soon as possible and I'll send out the orders."

After the meeting breaks up, you stay behind to make a list of names. Top of the list is Gagnon the navigator. Then Dagma for muscle, Piver for his mining experience and good humor, Shoola for her skill with a mountain sledge and Drexel for his climbing skills. You will make up the sixth member of the group. You only hope the

Lowlander troops will be able to keep up.

You hand the list to the chief. "I'm going to go to the equipment bay and start sorting out the sledges."

The chief smiles. "I'm pleased you're so eager to get on with the job." He glances down at the list. "I'll have everyone assemble in two days. If the weather is okay, you can leave that morning."

Two days will come around before you know it and you've got lots to do. "Piver and Gagnon are here at the Pillars, chief, I'll go tell them myself if that's okay. We can start planning right away."

The chief gives you a salute, "Off you go and remember, have a plan B. Even good plans can go wrong on the Black Slopes."

As you make your way to the cable lift, you wonder what you've got yourself into. When you reach level 8 you leap off and head down a corridor.

You find the little engineer fiddling with a piece of equipment on the workbench in front of him when you enter his pod.

"What's that?" you ask. "Some new invention?"

"Well hullo to you too," he says.

After you've bumped elbows in greeting, Piver grins, picks up the contraption and slots his fingers through its grip. Then he clips a strap around his wrist, points the tube end at the ceiling and pulls a trigger.

With a sharp hiss a tiny anchor bolt shoots up and

embeds itself in the smooth rock overhead. Then, with the whirl of a battery pack, Piver is lifted off the ground and reeled up a fine cable towards the ceiling.

"Weeeeeeeee…" Piver says as he rises higher and higher.

You look up. "What are you doing?"

Piver thumbs the release and comes zipping back down. "It's a pocket launcher. It's only got twenty feet of cable, but it'll be great for exploring the roofs of caves or creating a quick anchor if you're caught in the rain on a slippery slope. Here, have a look."

He hands you the launcher. "It's nice and light, I'll give you that."

Piver smiles. "The battery pack is built into the handle."

"How many lifts before you need to recharge?"

"Twenty or so. Unless you're a heavyweight hydro-gobbler like Dagma."

"Could you make a dozen of these in a couple days?" you ask.

"Sure, they're not complicated," Piver says. "Why?"

"Because we're going to Mount Kakona."

Piver lets out a high pitched giggle.

"Why are you laughing?" you ask.

"You're joking aren't you?" Piver's eyes search your face. When he doesn't see you smiling they go wide, the whites showing all around his dark green pupils.

"Geebus! You're serious!"

"We're going on a mining expedition. Command needs tyranium crystals in a hurry and they think Mount Kakona is where we'll find them."

"But that area's never been explored ... and it's active."

"A good reason to get in, harvest some crystals and get out as quickly as possible."

"Geebus, I hope you know what you're doing."

So do you, but you don't tell Piver that. "At least the old troop will be together again. I'm off to tell Gagnon now."

"Wait, before you go," Piver says. "Why does a red-beaked pango lift up one leg while it's sleeping?"

You know this is going to be bad, but you play along. "I don't know, Piver. Why?"

"Because if it lifts up both legs, it falls over!" Piver laughs like he's the one who made up the old joke.

Your eyes roll. "I see your material hasn't improved." You shake your head and chuckle. "Bye, Piver. Get onto those launchers. We leave for Mount Kakona in two days."

Piver's giggling follows you down the corridor. He may be a nutty little fellow, but you know from previous experience he's far braver than others realize, and smarter too.

You come to a set of steps cut into the rock wall. Two

flights down you find Gagnon exactly where you expected him to be, in the map room, studying.

"What is it with you and this place? You must have all of Petron memorized by now."

Gagnon looks up and smiles. "A good navigator needs to know his way around. Let me guess, we're off to Mount Kakona."

"How the heck do you know that? It's only just been decided by council."

"I was asked by the chief a week ago if I thought it was possible to navigate a route to Kakona's southern vents. I'm guessing they're after tyranium?"

"I'm impressed, Gagnon. I always knew you were clever. And yes, tyranium needle crystals, seems there's a desperate shortage."

"So are you leading the expedition or just recruiting?"

"Leading. We set off in two days." You lean over his shoulder. "How's the route looking?"

"Like a steaming bucket of pango poo, but I've got an idea."

"A good one I hope."

Gagnon smiles. "Could we take a medium sized driller along? I know they're heavy, and it would mean we'd be able to carry fewer supplies, but we could save five days travel and a lot of risk by tunneling through the Tyron Cliffs."

"Through the cliffs?"

"See here," he says, pointing to a long line marked on the map. "These cliffs are pretty risky to climb and even trickier to get around. Crevasse fields below and overhanging buttresses above. But, I've spotted a section where the cliffs are only 30 yards thick. About ten hours drilling I figure."

You know from geography class that this wall of shimmering black rock, pushed up by a series of big quakes thousands of years ago, is over 100 miles long. Those who have seen them say they are one of Petron's natural wonders. But they are also a big headache for anyone wanting to travel west and are the main reason the Kakona volcanic field hasn't been explored.

You think hard about what Gagnon has said. "Is that our best option?"

"The shortest distance between two points is a straight line," Gagnon says. "It's either that or a five day detour with the sledges across some incredibly dangerous country."

You stare at the map a while longer. "If we're loaded with crystals on the way back I suppose a tunnel would make good sense. We can ditch the mining gear too. Plus we'll have Lowlanders with us. Not sure they're up to a big climb."

But a medium sized driller will reduce the amount of food and other equipment you'll be able to take on the journey. And what if the driller breaks down before you get through? Either option has its risks.

It is time to make a decision Do you:

Take the drilling machine along? **P15**

Or

Take more food and equipment and leave the driller behind? **P26**

You have decided to suggest someone with more experience leads the expedition.

"I appreciate your confidence in me," you say. "But surely there is someone more qualified?"

The chief gives you a stern look. "Leadership isn't always about experience. It's also about attitude and having troopers that will follow you even when things get tough. In the past you've shown you can think fast and improvise when necessary. Valuable skills for a Slider Corps leader."

"And we trust you," the Lowland general adds. "You've spent time getting to know us and I believe you'll look after our interests fairly."

Heads are nodding all around the table.

You think hard for a reason to back out, but can't find one. Everyone is depending on you. And a trip to the interior will be exciting. You thump the table and nod. "Okay. I'll do it. Where are we going?"

"Ah, that's the tricky part," the chief says. "We want you to go to Crater Canyon."

"Crater Canyon? I always thought Crater Canyon was a myth. Are you telling me it actually exists?"

"Members of the council have always thought the canyon was a myth too, until a miner turned up raving about a huge vein of tyranium he'd found. Problem is, the miner seemed a bit unstable. He talked of huge snakes, robot hummingbirds, metallic spiders and strange people living near the hull of a huge, metal, bird-like craft."

"So why don't you get this miner to lead you back to where he found the crystals?"

The chief shakes his head. "We would … but he's gone missing."

"Missing?"

"Yes, just disappeared in the night. One witness claimed a flying disk picked him up and carried him away. Trackers tried to follow his scent up the mountain, but it faded to nothing after a hundred yards where they found small traces of an unidentified dust and burn marks on the rock. The whole thing was most unusual."

You scratch your head and think. "But if the miner was crazy, how do you know he found tyranium?"

The chief reaches down under the table and brings out a lump of rock. "Because he had this with him. Analysis shows it to be ninety-five percent pure. Our best mines only ever produced eighty percent."

The chief puts some papers on the table. "He also left these hand-drawn maps."

You walk around the table to have a look.

The chief points to a spot on the map. "We think this is Mount Transor, but it's unclear. The rest of the map looks like it covers an area on the other side of the main range."

"But the interior is totally unexplored," you say, wondering what you've got yourself into. "And if the miner was mentally unstable…"

The Lowland general clears his throat. "Just because the miner's kooky doesn't mean everything he said was wrong. I mean tiny metal birds and huge snakes sound a bit unlikely, but look at that rock. Have you ever seen such tightly bunched crystals?"

You have to admit you haven't. "They seem much finer than usual too."

The chief rubs his hand lightly over the specimen. "You could just about walk up wet rock if you had these on the soles of your boots. Imagine if we found the main source and what a difference it would make to our ability to move around the slopes. Imagine not worrying about sliding to the bottom every time there's a light shower, or in the evenings after dewfall?"

The chief's eyes are gleaming with excitement. He makes a good point. This quality of needle crystals would change life on the Black Slopes forever. And you've got a chance to be part of history.

"When do we leave?" you say with a smile, accepting the challenge. "I've always wondered what the interior is like."

"Great," the chief says. "I knew you'd come around. The only thing left to decide is if you take a big well-equipped group, or one that's smaller and faster."

It is time for you to make a decision. Do you:

Go for a big well-equipped group? **P34**

Or:

Go for a smaller yet faster group? **P45**

You have decided to take the driller and try to drill through the Tyron Cliffs.

"Geebus this thing is heavy," Piver says as he swings one end of the drill onto the sledge. "I hope this works. Otherwise we'll be humping this along for nothing."

Piver's right. It is a risk. But you trust Gagnon's ability to pinpoint the exact spot to drill. If he's more than ten yards off in either direction, or gets the angle wrong you'll be drilling for two days rather than ten hours, and two days drilling without a replacement bit is one and a half days too many.

"Just make sure you load everything we'll need for twelve hours drilling and leave the tactics up to Gagnon," you say as you help Piver with the other end of the bulky machine. "When has he let us down before?"

The two of you go back to loading up the second sledge with boxes of dried hydro and premixed containers of broth. Then you add a burner for cooking, fuel, extra harnesses, anchor guns, spare cable and plenty of battery powered zippers.

There will be no tows or formed paths on the other side of the Tyron Cliffs. All climbing will be done with portable tow launchers and zip lines and the sliding will be slow and difficult. When the batteries run out, you'll have to climb like Highlanders did in the old days, with leg power, skill and determination.

The next two days go in a flurry of work and organization. When departure day arrives, you are frantically checking lists of equipment and stores.

The chief has come down to introduce you to the Lowland members of the expedition. "This is Trodie, he's the ranking Lowland officer and their best climber," the chief says. "All the Lowlanders have had cross country experience so they should be well matched to your troop."

The chief gives you a wink as he says this. He knows no Lowlanders can match the Slider Corp for traveling on the Black Slopes, but he doesn't want to embarrass Trodie in front of his troop.

Trodie is a head taller than you and stocky in build. The guide stick he's carrying looks awkward in his hand. The two of you bump elbows and then turn back to the chief.

"Trodie is to be second in command. I suggest you work together to make this expedition a success. Forget that some of you are Lowlanders and others are Highlanders. Just remember you are all Petronians and treat each other with respect."

The chief salutes and then heads back down the corridor towards the lift.

"Okay everyone," you say. "Let's get our harnesses on and these sledges hooked up. We've got one big tow to the top ridge and then a long slide to the end of the

Western Track. After that we leave the tracks behind."

Your troop wastes no time in hooking up to the sledges. Dagma and Shoola take their customary places at the rear where they will act as brakes. Gagnon and Drexel hook their harnesses to the steering runners at the front.

Gagnon looks at Drexel. "Just as well we replaced the diamond grit on our runners last week eh? I suspect we'll need every bit of grip we can get."

Drexel pats the anchor gun hanging on his utility belt. "Quick draw's my specialty. I don't plan on going to the bottom this trip."

You turn to Trodie. "Put a Lowlander on the back of each sledge to help with the breaking. You and I will lead. Everyone else can ride on the sledges for now. We'll reorganize things once we get to the Tyron Cliffs."

Within minutes your group is ready to hook on to the 3000 foot tow that will take you up to the high ridge overlooking the Pillars of Haramon.

The high-tensile cable hums as it runs up the slick towpath. Those who are sliding swivel the lock bar out of their front boot and clip it into a fitting on the instep of their back boot to form a stable sliding platform.

Rows of tiny diamonds on their soles give the sliders some steering ability and a diamond spur on the heel of their back boot provides some stopping power. The sliders push forward with the needle end of their guide sticks and get ready to clamp onto the tow.

"On my mark," you yell. "Three, two, one…"

With knees bent, you swing your clamp over the cable and press down hard. As the clamp grips the cable you start moving up the towpath. Leaning back into your harness you concentrate on keeping your balance. You can't think of a worse way to start an expedition than to have its leader slip and fall over on the first tow.

Gagnon and Dagma's sledge is right behind you, while Drexel and Shoola's brings up the rear.

As you look back down the towline, the Lowlanders seem to be coping with the challenge of the towpath so far. You just hope they've got some traversing skills too. Sliding on formed paths is one thing, but free sliding in unknown terrain is another matter altogether.

When you reach the top of the tow, you release your clamp and slide along the offloading platform. The screech of diamonds sound across the ridge as everyone comes to a stop.

You love the feel of a guide stick in your hand. It's almost an extension of your arms. A blue diamond hook is mounted at one end for stopping and a thick pad of tyranium needle crystals are fixed to the other for steering and pushing. A guide stick and glide boots are the two items of equipment that no member of the Highland Slider Corps can do without.

The Pillars of Haramon are now far below. Light bounces off their reflective surfaces making them glisten, dark and foreboding, in the soft morning light.

To the west is the volcanic plateau. The air up this high is clean and cool. Nearly a hundred miles in the distance the black cone of Mount Kakona towers above the mountains around it. This is going to be a tricky expedition. Kakona's western vents are halfway up the mountain's flank. But climbing Mount Kakona is the least of your worries. First you have to get to its base.

"So what do you think Gagnon? Are we going to make it there and back before our food runs out?"

Gagnon has a look of quiet confidence. "My calculations say we can. If not we'll just have to eat wild pangos."

Trodie and Piver slide over to where you and Gagnon are talking. Trodie is mumbling under his breath.

"Sorry what's that?" you ask.

"I'm just trying to convince myself I'm not dreaming. I've looked up at these mountains all my life and now that I'm here amongst them. I feel so small."

You know how Trodie feels. Every time you come up here you feel the same.

Trodie points towards Mount Kakona. "Is that it? The one we're going to?"

Piver shakes his head. "Nah, Mount Kakona's much bigger than that, you can't even see it from here."

Trodie's jaw drops, "Wha...?"

"Ha! Got ya!" Piver says erupting into hysterical

giggling. "How could a mountain get any bigger than that monster?"

"Hey, Piver, I thought I told you not to tease the Lowlanders," you say, trying not to smile.

Trodie grins. "I just hope you know how to take a joke too, funny man. Phew, you had me worried there."

"I'd still be worried if I was you," Gagnon says. "Climbing the volcano might be the easy part. We've got to get there first, then there's the small matter of Mount Kakona being active."

"I hear that hot rock is hard on the boots," Piver say looking at Trodie. "Melts right through the soles in minutes."

Trodie's mouth drops again.

Then Piver starts laughing again. "Geebus, you Lowlanders are gullible, if the rock's hot, you go around it."

You give Piver a sharp look. "Stop it, Piver!"

"You'll keep my little friend," Trodie says, wagging his finger and smiling. "You'll keep."

"We'd better get moving if we're going to make it to the Tyron Cliffs by dewfall," you say. "Gagnon, what's our first traverse like?"

Gagnon explains the route he's planned. "The Western Track's narrow but at least it's a track. It's 40 miles and three zips up to the head of Black Gully."

Dagma is acting as brake on the heaviest sledge with

the drilling machine. Shoola has the lighter supply sledge. You notice both the girls are munching on hydro bars to keep their energy levels up.

"Eyes open and knees bent," you tell everyone. "We don't want any accidents today. Dagma let me know if you need extra help with that sledge. No playing the hero."

With that, you and Trodie lead the troop off the platform and onto the grade 2 track. The first traverse takes you due west towards the head of Black Gully. Every ten miles or so, you'll need to launch a cable and zip up to gain more altitude. This will enable you to keep traversing along the well-worn track notched into the side of the mountainside.

Then, once you've reached Black Gully, it's a twenty-mile slide down to the drill site on the spectacular Tyron Cliffs.

With your guide stick tucked under your arm and both hands firmly on its shaft, you point your front foot downhill and push off. As you slide, you hear the faint swish of Trodie's boots gliding across the rock behind you.

It's times like this that you enjoy being a slider the most, the wind rushing past your visor, the soft hiss of boots on black glass. The view out to the sea and the smell of the mountains make you feel alive.

After the first ten-mile traverse, the cable launcher is

set up and Drexel fires an anchor bolt into the ridge high above. Once you've all zipped up to the next section of track, you lead off on another traverse further west.

A range of sharp peaks runs from east to west. Your group runs parallel to them. A few wisps of cloud can be seen beyond their peaks to the south, but thankfully none have crossed the divide onto your side of the range. Rain is the one danger all Highlanders fear. It can turn an easily traversable slope into an ultra-slick nightmare in seconds. Even eighty percent tyranium crystals won't hold on a slope of more than ten degrees on wet rock.

After a long and tiring slide, you and your troop reach the top of Black Gully. You call a halt on a small patch of level ground and look down the narrow chute. It's easy to see why it got its name. Black Gully is a natural half-pipe with curved wave-like overhangs on both sides. Because it runs north to south, very little natural light gets down into its depths, making the gully almost look like a tunnel at certain times of the day. Deep shadows hide the gully's many irregularities and make it a far trickier place to slide than it looks.

"Don't let this innocent looking place catch you out," you say to the group. "Black Gully's known for its sudden dips and ripples so keep your hooks at the ready and your knees bent. It's also an area where WAVs are known to roll, so stay alert."

"I forgot you had those up here." Trodie says

nervously, looking up towards the peaks above.

You nod. "They start life up here. Wild pango's eat the seeds of the Wandering Adamus Vines, or WAVs as we call them and then poop them out near their breeding colonies. Some of the seeds sprout in the nutrients that collect under the pango colonies and as the WAVs grow they become these big ugly 100 pound balls of thorns. Eventually they get too heavy for their tiny roots to hold them on the slope and they roll off downhill."

"I know," Trodie says. "They come bouncing down the mountain at high speed until they reach the Lowlands. We have villagers injured by them every summer in the high pastures."

"I bet that hurts," Piver says.

"You're not wrong there," Trodie say. "I suppose you sliders get a few injuries too."

You nod. "They come from nowhere sometimes. The only warning is a dry rustling sound. Best just to lay flat and hope they roll over you without leaving too many thorns behind. If you try to run, they can knock you right off the mountain."

"I know a girl who got prickled good n' proper," Piver says. "You should have seen her afterwards. What a mess."

Trodie looks worried. "I've heard rumors these plants can think. Any truth in that?"

You shrug. "I've heard that too. An old man in my

community said he saw a WAV change into the shape of an animal and run on four legs. But he was a bit happy on moth mist at the time so he was probably dreaming. The main thing is to get through Black Gully as quickly as possible and, if you do see a WAV coming, hit the deck, grit your teeth and cross your fingers."

You gesture for the group to move out and lead them down into Black Gully on a safe route that uses the natural contours of the half pipe to slow you down as you swoop from one side to the other.

"Whoopee!" Piver yells from the top on one of the sledge. "Go faster you slowpokes!"

Some of the Lowlanders aren't so happy riding on the weaving sledges. One in particular is suffering from motion sickness.

"Maybe a raw pango egg would help settle your stomach," Piver tells him.

"Eurghhh!" the Lowlander says, losing his lunch.

"Piver, stop it!" you say over your shoulder. "I told you to play nice."

"Geebus did you see that?" Piver says. "That looked nasty!"

With an empty stomach, the young Lowlander feels better within minutes. As your group exits Black Gully, you come onto a plateau and see the Tyron Cliffs spread before you. Immediately all thoughts, except those of utter amazement, are forgotten.

'Holy moly,' someone behind you says.

'Geebus!' Piver squeaks. "Look at 'em."

The cliffs rise vertically, shimmering black and almost translucent. You are so lost in their beauty that you almost forget you're in charge of the expedition.

"Tether your sledges," you say. "Remember everything slips on black glass, even on the slightest of slopes. If you don't want to lose it, tie it down."

The sun is low. You have about an hour before dewfall when the slopes will become treacherous. You could set up the driller ready for an early start in the morning, or you could set up camp and leave the driller for the morning.

It would be nice to start drilling early, the more time you save the longer your supplies will last, but you also know everyone is tired from the days travel and setting it up will mean more work.

It is time to make a decision. Do you:

Set the drill up ready for the morning? **P52**

Or

Set up camp first in case the weather turns? **P57**

You have decided to take more food and equipment and leave the driller behind.

"I'd rather go around the cliffs," you say to Gagnon. "We might starve to death if we take a two hundred pound drill rather than food with us. And what if the thing breaks down? What then?"

"But—?"

"Look, if we can find a way around the Tyron Cliffs. A track can be built and others will be able to follow. That will open up a whole new area."

"But it's never been done before. And going around is quite a distance."

You shrug. "There has to be a first time. Besides, who knows what interesting discoveries we'll make along the way."

Gagnon isn't all that happy, but then you are the expedition leader and the decisions are yours to make.

The next two days go in a flurry of work and organization. When departure day arrives you are frantically checking lists of equipment and stores.

The chief has come down to introduce you to the Lowland members of the expedition. "This is Trodie, he's the ranking Lowland officer and their best climber."

The chief gives you a wink as he says this. He knows full well no Lowlanders can match the Slider Corp for traveling on the Black Slopes, but he doesn't want to embarrass Trodie in front of his troop. Trodie is a head taller than you and stocky in build.

"Carry on." The chief salutes and then heads back down the corridor towards the lift.

"Okay everyone," you say. "Let's get our harnesses on and these sledges hooked up. We've got one big tow to the top ridge and then a long slide to the end of the Western Track. After that we leave the tracks behind."

Your troop wastes no time in hooking up to the sledges. Dagma and Shoola take their customary places at the rear where they will act as brakes. Gagnon and Drexel hook their harnesses to the steering runners at the front.

You turn to Trodie. "Your team can ride on the sledges for now. You and I will lead."

Within minutes your group is ready to clamp on to the 3000-foot-long tow that will take you up to the high ridge overlooking the Pillars of Haramon.

The high-tensile cable vibrates as it runs up the slick towpath. Those who are sliding swivel the lock bar out of their front boot and clip it into a fitting on the instep of their back boot to form a stable sliding platform.

Rows of tiny diamonds on the soles of their boots give sliders some steering ability, and diamond spurs on their heels provides some stopping power. The sliders push forward with the needle end of their guide sticks and get ready to clamp onto the tow.

"On my mark," you yell. "Three, two, one…"

With knees bent, you swing your clamp over the cable and press down hard. As the clamp bites onto the cable, you are dragged up the towpath. You lean back into your harness and concentrate on keeping your balance.

Gagnon and Dagma's sledge is right behind you, while Drexel and Shoola's sledge brings up the rear.

When you reach the top of the tow, you release your clamp and slide along the offloading platform. The screech of diamonds sound across the ridge as everyone comes to a stop.

The guide stick in your hand is almost an extension of your arm. A blue diamond hook is mounted at one end for stopping and a thick pad of tyranium needle crystals are fixed to the other for steering and pushing.

To the east are the volcanoes.

"Quite a sight, eh, Gagnon?"

Gagnon nods. "I'm looking forward to the view from up there, back towards home. Should be even better."

You smile at his confidence. "Especially with a sledge load of tyranium."

Trodie and Piver slide over to where you and Gagnon are talking.

Trodie points towards the east, where one mountain towers over the others. "That must be Kakona."

"That's it. Hope you brought your climbing legs along," you say.

"Does the volcano normally glitter like that?" Trodie

says.

You are about to answer, when you see a disk-shaped light near Kakona's summit. "What is that?"

Piver pulls out his scope and trains it on the glint in the distance. "It's moving whatever it is."

As the rest of you look on. The light moves off towards the interior.

"Could be a meteorite," Piver says.

"Moving a bit slow for one of those, isn't it?" Gagnon asks. "And since when do they glow silver?"

When the light disappears behind the range of mountains, everyone is left shaking their heads.

"Or it could have been some strange atmospheric condition, or reflected lights from over the horizon," Piver says.

"Lights from the interior you mean?" you say. "Where it's uninhabited?"

Piver shrugs. "Anything's possible."

"Lowlanders have seen lights in the sky before," Trodie says. "Some say it's visitors from another planet."

You look at Trodie. "Those are just stories in the *Book of Myths* aren't they?"

Piver giggles nervously. "Let's hope so."

"Anyway, it's gone now so let's get moving," you say.

Gagnon explains the route he's planned. "The Western Track's narrow but at least it's a track. We've got a long traverse and we'll need to zip up a few times before we get to the head of Black Gully."

Dagma and Shoola look keen to get going and are stomping their feet in an effort to keep their leg muscles warm.

"Eyes open and knees bent," you say. "We have a long way to slide."

With that, you and Trodie lead the troop off the platform and onto the grade-two track. The first traverse takes you due west towards the head of Black Gully. With every yard forward, you lose a little altitude. Every ten miles or so, you need to launch a cable and zip up to gain more height to enable you to keep traversing.

Then, once you've reached Black Gully, it's a twenty-mile slide down to the spectacular Tyron Cliffs.

With your guide stick tucked under your arm and both hands firmly on its shaft, you point your front foot slightly downhill and push off. You hear the faint swish of Trodie's boots sliding across the rock behind you.

"Whoopee!" Piver yells. "Giddy up you guys, I want to see these cliffs everyone keeps talking about."

After the first ten mile traverse, the cable launcher is set up and an anchor bolt is fired into the ridge high above. Once you've all zipped up to the next section of track, you lead off on another traverse further west.

The Black Slopes run from east to west in a series of peaks. Your group runs parallel to them. A few wisps of faint purple mist can be seen beyond their peaks, but thankfully none have crossed the divide onto your side of the range. Rain on slippery black rock is the last thing you need.

After a long slide, you and your troop reach the top of Black Gully. You call a halt on a small patch of level ground and look down the narrow passage. It's easy to see how Black Gully got its name. The gully is a natural half-pipe of rock with curved wave-like overhangs on both sides. These overhangs thin out as they rise, leaving crests of black glass you can almost see through.

"It's beautiful," Trodie says.

"Don't let this innocent looking place catch you out," you say. "Black Gully's known for its sudden dips and ripples so keep your hook at the ready and your knees bent."

"I was born with my hook ready," Dagma says, eager to go. "Now let's tame this beast!"

The route down Black Gully is a series of sweeping S-turns that uses the natural contours of the half pipe to slow the sledges down.

"Whoopee!" Piver yells from the top on one of them. "Let's have a race!"

"Race!" Dagma yells over the wind. "I love going fast."

Shoola picks up speed. "Woot, woot!"

The sledges whizz up one side and down the other, back and forth, up and down. Occasionally, a sudden dip has the sledges airborne for a moment.

"That's more like it!" Piver yells. "Woot! Woot! Go sliders!"

Time passes quickly when you're having fun and it isn't long before you come out of Black Gully and back into open country. It's then that you see the Tyron Cliffs towering before you for the first time. All thoughts, except those of utter amazement, are forgotten.

"Geebus!" Piver squeaks. "Now that was worth waiting for."

The cliffs rise vertically, shimmering black and semi-translucent. Another two hundred yards and your group comes to a stop at the foot of the cliffs.

Standing stock still, not a member of the group is able to take their eyes off them. You are so lost in their beauty that you almost forget you're in charge.

"Tether your sledges," you say. "I don't want to lose any gear."

The sun is low. It's only an hour before dewfall when dampness makes the slopes treacherous. "Get the burners set up, and sling your hammocks," you tell the crew. "We'll make camp here tonight."

Then finally, after a hot cup of broth, you climb into your hammock and take the weight off your feet. In minutes you sink into a deep sleep.

When you wake the next morning, the sky is clear and a light easterly is blowing. As you sit around a burner having your morning broth, Gagnon comes and sits beside you.

"So are we going uphill or downhill to try and find a way around this thing?" Gagnon asks. "I'll need to start planning a route."

"Any advantage in one over the other?" you ask.

Gagnon pulls a map out of his pocket and rests it on his knee. "The downhill terrain looks a lot easier, but we'll have to climb back up. Uphill, looks a lot tougher, but we'll gain some altitude and end up a little closer to Kakona. All in all, it's fifty-fifty I'd say."

Gagnon hasn't really helped. Fifty-fifty is just that, a coin toss. You are a little worried about the Lowlanders handling the rougher terrain if you go up, but then will they handle a long climb back up if you go down?

It is time to trust your gut. Do you:

Go up and around the Tyron Cliffs? **P157**

Or

Go down and around the Tyron Cliffs? **P167**

34

You have decided to go for a big well-equipped expedition.

You can't believe you've just agreed to lead an expedition to Crater Canyon.

"I think an expedition of this importance requires a big, well equipped troop," you say, studying the chief's reaction to your decision. "We'll have to cut steps, and use zip lines once we leave the Highland tracks behind. And in the event that there are unexpected dangers in the interior, we'll need quite a few sliders for protection."

"My thoughts exactly," the chief says. "Two sledges rather than one, six per sledge. One slider steering, two braking, and three riding onboard, all fully loaded with launchers, zip lines, portable tows, burners and supplies for a month."

"We'll need one of the Lowlander's step cutting machines too," you say looking over at the general. "I hear you've made them small enough to be sledge mounted. Is that true?"

"Err ... um, news travels fast." The Lowland general is a little surprised at your knowledge of their new step cutting technology, but after a moment's hesitation he puffs out his chest. "As you know, our original machines were big, steam powered things. Unfortunately, they were slow and cumbersome and vulnerable to attack. As you Highlanders discovered when you sent a couple to the bottom during the conflicts a few years ago. Since the truce we've learned much and have made many improvements. Our new cutters can be carried by sledge or even short distances by a strong person should the need arise."

"General," you say. "One of those new cutters and someone who knows how to operate it would be a huge help on this mission."

The general chats to one of his advisors and then nods. "I'll get one sent up right away. My eldest son, Villum, can come with you to operate it."

You're not so sure you want the general's son along on the expedition. Will he expect special treatment? And what happens if he is harmed in some way. Could his injury put the fragile truce with the Lowlanders in jeopardy? You are about to suggest the general's son train one of your miners to operate the step cutter when the chief buts in.

"Good idea, General. Your son can be second in charge."

Your mouth is left hanging open as you look questioningly at the chief. Why has he made this decision without consulting you, the expedition leader?

After the meeting has finished, you pull the chief aside. "What was that all about, chief? The general's son? Second in charge? Are you sure that's a good idea?"

"Look," the chief says. "We need to keep the

Lowlanders happy. If they feel ignored on this expedition they might decide to mount one of their own. These new step cutters give them the ability to move around the mountains as never before. And as every member of the Slider Corp knows, mobility is power when it comes to controlling the Black Slopes."

"Okay but—"

"Listen," the chief says, cutting you off. "While you're away, I need you to get your most trusted engineer to learn all there is to know about these machines. Our diamond drillers do the job but they are too darn slow and can overheat. We need to discover what it is about their machine that gives it the ability to do the job so quickly. Do you understand?"

You still don't like the idea, but you don't really have much choice. "Okay, Chief."

The chief walks to a window and looks down Long Gully to the Lowlands below. "There have been some disturbing rumors from the Borderlands about the Lowlanders stockpiling weapons," he whispers. "We need this technology and we need it now. If the truce fails and we end up having to protect the Highlands from invasion we're going to struggle without it."

By the look on the chief's face he's worried. The communities of the Black Slopes rely on him and the council to make the best decision for all of the Highlands. If he's worried about the Lowlanders breaking the truce, you are too.

"Okay Chief, I'll get Piver onto it as soon as we depart. He's far brighter than anyone realizes and one of the best engineers around. People tend to underestimate him. If anyone can work out how these Lowland cutters work, it's him."

The chief pulls a star out of his pocket and pins it onto your tunic. "Just in case anyone forgets who's in charge. Remember, I'm relying on you."

You look down at the star and try to keep your smile to a minimum. "Thanks, Chief."

"Now," the chief says, brushing a spot of dust off your jacket. "I'd better get back to playing host. You go get your troop organized. You leave in two days."

After leaving the command pod your first task is to find the little engineer.

"Piver," you say once you locate him in one of the workshops. "I want you to organize the equipment we'll need for the journey while I concentrate on logistics and communications."

"It's a wonder you can concentrate on anything with that rock sparkling in your face," Piver smirks, indicating the diamond on your tunic."

"I bet you're not laughing so much when we head off for Crater Canyon."

"Geebus!" Piver says, with a gulp "Crater Canyon? I thought that place was a myth."

You explain about the lump of tyranium the chief showed you and tell him about the slightly mad miner's vanishing act.

Piver grins. "So that's a definite maybe then."

"Yep," you say enjoying Piver's little joke. "A definite maybe if ever I saw one."

"I'd better get to work then," Piver says, turning back to his workbench. "I've just finished a new prototype launcher. This trip will be the perfect place to test it."

The next two days are a blur of packing and organization. When departure day arrives, it feels like you've been at it non-stop for weeks.

Two sledges and their personnel are assembled at the bottom of the first tow.

As the high-tensile cable hums up the towpath the sliders hook up their harnesses. Being inexperienced at traversing the tricky mountain paths, the Lowland general's son, Villum, and his assistant will ride aboard the second sledge carrying their step cutting machine, as will Piver.

The ride to the top of the first tow goes without a hitch. From there your plan is to go west, following the Western Track as far as you can. After the track peters out, all you'll have are the rough maps made by the kooky miner to follow.

At the first meal break, you and Gagnon, the expedition's navigator, sit beside one another with hot cups of broth.

"I've been comparing the miner's maps with some of our own." Gagnon says. "Thankfully he's marked a few landmarks we already know about. At least they should give us a reference point."

"Well if anyone is going to be able to decipher them, it's you, Gagnon."

"The bad news is that we've got to get over Tyron Pass."

"Yikes," you say. "That's a big climb."

"And it'll be a long slide down the other side too," Gagnon says before draining the last of his broth. "Let's just hope it's not too steep. Not much is known about that area."

The next two days are spent sliding west, launching cables, zipping up and then sliding west once more in a series of long, slow traverses.

On the first day of the expedition, the towering Mount Tyron never seemed to get any closer, but now that you're nearer, every step you take makes the mountain loom ever closer.

Villum spends much of his time napping on Dagma's sledge, atop his treasured step cutting machine. It's only when your troop reaches a steep pitch, where there's nothing to launch a anchor bolt into, that you're forced to wake him and ask him to fire up the step cutter.

"Again, already?" Villum moans. "All this climbing's

giving me a headache."

You roll your eyes at Piver and then turn to the general's son. "Come on, the quicker we cut the steps the sooner you can get back to your nap."

You remind yourself to give the chief a kick in the bum when you get back to the Pillars. What a pillock he's saddled you with. He should have known better than to take a highborn Lowlander on an expedition like this.

Thankfully the step cutting machine works a lot harder than Villum. Once set up and started, the machine's front-mounted cutting bit drills an oval hole in the hard black rock, then ratchets forwards and does it again, all at walking pace.

It's hard work climbing the steps, finding an anchor point, then winching the sledges up afterwards, but your troop soon finds a rhythm and the work goes smoothly. Everyone works hard, except Villum, who expects to walk up without having to carry anything, and then complains that he's tired.

Dagma's at the end of her patience when she pulls you aside. "Permission to send this bleating LoLa to the bottom."

"If he wasn't the general's son, I'd be tempted to say permission granted. Unfortunately this particular LoLa needs to get back to the Pillars in one piece."

Dagma grunts under her breath and gets back to work. Piver hears her grumbling and wanders over.

You take a couple of paces towards them so you can eavesdrop. You know Piver and suspect he's up to mischief.

"Hey Dagma," Piver says. "What's soft and lazy and smells like pango poo?"

"Smells like pango poo? How the heck should I know?" Dagma grumps.

Piver nods to where Villum is sitting against a small pinnacle rising from the surrounding slope. Above his head roost a dozen or so red-beaked pangos.

Dagma looks confused.

"Try this riddle then," Piver says. "What bird poops like crazy whenever they're frightened?"

Dagma looks at Villum, then at the birds above him and smiles at Piver. "You're not as stupid as you look funny man."

"And what scares a pango?" Piver asks Dagma.

"Absolutely everything!" the two Highlanders say in unison before exploding with peals of laughter.

You chuckle under your breath. At least Piver's made Dagma stop grumbling for a moment.

Dagma pulls out her slingshot and drops a small stone in its pouch. With a quick pull, she sends the stone whizzing towards the roosting birds.

"Erk! Erk!" the birds squawk, pooping as they fly off.

Villum screams in horror as a fishy mess comes splattering down all over him, then he jumps to his feet, unsure of whether to wipe the stinky stuff off with his hand or not.

Piver and Dagma watch Villum's discomfort and hoot with laughter. You turn your back and smirk, trying your best not to let Villum see that you're laughing at him as well.

Eventually, when he manages to stop himself from giggling, Piver slides over and tosses Villum a piece of cloth. "Here use this. It'll take the worst of it off."

Dagma shoulders another load of equipment and starts up the most recently cut steps with an extra bounce in her step.

"Okay everyone," you say to your troop. "One more pitch and we're at the pass. It's all downhill from there. Now I know you're tired, but keep going. We need to find a safe place to camp on the other side before dewfall."

As you climb you can't help thinking of all the possible dangers you'll face in the interior. You also wonder how accurate the miner's maps are. Will there be a safe way down to Crater Canyon and this newly discovered vein of tyranium? Will any of the wild claims made by the miner be true? Will there be snakes or mechanical creatures?

From the pass a whole new world spread before you. The other side, near the top, is bare rock, just like what you've been climbing. But further down the mountain, the interior is lush and green. In the distance, an emerald lake shimmers in the last of the afternoon sun.

"Not quite so steep this side," Gagnon says with relief looking through his scope. "I see a couple of possible ways down."

You pull out your own scope and take a look. "Anything look familiar from the miner's maps?"

"One thing," Gagnon says, raising his arm and pointing towards a hill to the west of the lake. "See that volcano? According to the miner, Crater Canyon's near the base of a volcano. That could be it."

Gagnon looks west and shields his eyes from the sun as it dips near the horizon. "We've only got an hour to find somewhere to camp. We'd better get going."

"Harness up, Sliders," you say. "Single file, two brakes per sledge. And keep your speed down and hooks at the ready. Gagnon's sledge will take the lead."

You hear the screech of diamond studs and guide sticks as the sliders move into position.

"So," you say, looking at Gagnon. "Which way do you recommend?"

"I see two options," Gagnon says, pointing down the slope to his right. "There's a natural watercourse just over there. Seeing there's been no rain recently it's empty at the moment and should be passable for sledges. Or, we can go slightly west and zigzag down that broad ridge. Technically, the ridge is harder, but we'll get a better view of the surrounding territory and any possible dangers."

44

It is time to make a decision. Do you:

Go down the watercourse? **P63**

Or

Zigzag down the broad ridge? **P70**

You have decided to go for a smaller yet faster group.

"I like the idea of a small, fast group, with one sledge and extra muscle for the climbing."

The chief slaps you on the shoulder. "Good choice. Less crew to worry about and a reduced time on the slopes."

"We'll definitely need some extra leg power," you say. "Getting up to the pass isn't going to be easy."

As the chief and the other representatives get back to their discussions, you excuse yourself and get to work. If you're leaving in two days, there's planning to do.

First you'll need to contact Piver. His engineering and mining skills will be essential if this expedition is to be a success. You'll also want Gagnon as navigator, Dagma and Shoola for their muscle and sliding skills, and Drexel for climbing.

The Lowland general also wants you to take his representatives Trodie, and Villum the general's son, along. Bringing the total crew to eight members.

Eight is a couple more than a single sledge would normally accommodate, but if you all carry backpacks with the extra gear you'll need for a long journey, it shouldn't be a problem.

After speaking to Piver in his workshop on level four, you find Gagnon, in the map room, further down on level two.

You and Gagnon bump elbows in greeting.

"Feel like a trip?" you ask.

Gagnon smiles, "Crater Canyon by any chance?"

"How did you know that?"

"The chief was asking me questions about it the other day. I figured something was in the wind."

Gagnon always surprises you. He misses very little and is an expert at reading people.

"So is Crater Canyon real?" you ask him. "And if so, can we find it?"

Gagnon sits down at the map table again. You see he's been comparing a hand-drawn map with one drawn up by the Slider Corps.

"Is that the miner's map the chief was talking about?"

"It's a copy the chief gave me," Gagnon says. "From what I can tell, this mysterious miner was in the interior alright." Gagnon points to a spot on the map. "But I don't think this is to the west like everyone else thinks. I think this is much further east."

"East? Through the wild lands? I've heard rumors of strange creatures to the east."

"We can't let a few rumors stop us. And has anyone brought back proof of these monsters?"

You shake your head.

"Anyone can make up stories," Gagnon continues. "But without proof, why should we believe them?"

"Okay, I see your point. So what are you suggesting?"

"Rather than going up and over the mountains, I think we should slide fast and traverse around the eastern end of the Black Slopes. It may be a lot longer, but we'll be covering ground quickly and relatively safely. Besides, who knows what we'll find along the way."

After discussing the pros and cons, you decide to go along with Gagnon's idea and leave him to plan the route east while you go back to the accommodation pod to look for the others.

Shoola and Dagma are in the canteen stuffing their faces with hydro and broth. They are grunting between bites and arguing about who's the best brake on a sledge.

"I hate to break up your little party," you say, sitting down beside the two sliders. "But I've got a job for you."

Dagma slurps, then turns to face you. She looks interested. "Oh yeah?"

"You two might be able to settle who's best once and for all on this trip."

News of a trip is one of the few things that will take a hungry slider's mind off food. By the time you've explained what you need, you have their full attention.

Two days later, the sledge is loaded and all the organizing has come together. The chief watches from the command pod as you get ready to catch the first tow up to the ridge high above the Pillars.

The tow path is ultra-slick from particularly heavy dew so you get Gagnon and Drexel to attach their harnesses to the front of the sledge, while Dagma and Shoola to connect to the back.

As the front sliders clamp on to the whirling cable, the sledge starts to move up the slippery black rock. The sliders on the front make subtle adjustments to the steering runners to keep the sledge traveling in a straight line while those on the back get ready to drop their hooks should the sledge come adrift from the tow.

After offloading at the top, rather than turning left like so many other expeditions you've been on, you turn east and wonder what adventures this wild uncharted territory will bring.

"Well, this should be interesting," you say to the others. "Eastward ho on my mark. Three … two … one … slide!"

And with that, your group points their feet slightly downhill and traverses off across the slope. You are in the lead acting as scout. Then come the four sliders controlling the sledge. Riding on top of the sledge are Piver and the two Lowlanders, Trodie and Villum.

The rock on this part of the mountain is crevasse free so you make good time. On occasion you pass small pillars, the result of some long past eruption. Pangos have made these their nesting place, well above the marauding packs of morph rats that eat everything in their path.

Under these pillars, growing from seeds carried up

from the Lowlands by the pangos, are wild adamas vines, or WAV's as the Highlanders call them. These plants grow into tightly packed balls of thorns. But eventually, these thorny plants get too heavy for their shallow roots and they go rolling off down the mountain, bowling over and skewering anything in their path.

The first day goes by without any problems. About an hour before dewfall, you find a reasonably flat section of ground and make camp.

As you're warming yourself around the burner, enjoying a well earned meal, Gagnon tells you that the troop has covered nearly sixty miles. "That's got to be a record," he says.

You look towards home, now a fair distance away, and watch the sun dip behind Mt Transor. The sky is bright orange and red, but the sunset only lasts a brief moment. Once it's dark, you climb into your hammock and drift off to sleep, dreaming of black slopes and home.

At dawn you wake to clear skies. After a quick breakfast, everyone gets back into harness ready for the day's slide. Trodie, complaining of a sore bum from riding on the sledge the previous day, decides to slide. Piver does the same. Only Villum opts to ride.

As you slide off across the slope, Piver tucks himself into your slipstream and gives you a rundown on the two Lowlanders.

"Trodie's straight up," Piver says. "But that Villum,

what a stupid LoLa he is. Just complains about everything."

You've heard similar comments from others, but it's not like you could leave the general's son behind. He's one of the appointed Lowland representatives and you're stuck with him.

"Be patient, Piver. He's out of his comfort zone up here. He'll settle in."

"Or fall off the sledge while he's sleeping and go to the bottom."

"Piver! Enough of that talk. He's our responsibility. Play nice."

"Righto," the little engineer says. "Just don't ask me to like him."

Gagnon's travel plan is going well. When you stop for lunch on the second day he says the expedition's made another 32 miles. After eating, you climb up the slope a little ways to scope out the next run. As you focus on the black rock to the east, you see a bright, metallic disk sitting on the slope about a mile away.

You're not sure if you believe your eyes. "Hey, Gagnon! Come up here a moment."

"I see it!" Gagnon says. "It looks just like those pictures in the *Book of Myths*."

"Yeah. In those stories about the people from space."

"According to the *Book of Myths*," Gagnon says. "these disks were how our ancestors arrived on Petron. But they're supposed to be stories, not reality."

"Until now," you say.

"So what do we do?"

"That, my friend, is a very good question."

It is time to make a decision. What do you do? Do you.

Go check out the spaceship? **P176**

Or

Stay and observe the spaceship from a distance? **P182**

You have decided to set the drill up ready for the morning.

You've got a limited food supply and a long way to go. Your troop may be tired but every bit of time you save means you'll have a better chance of reaching your goal.

"Let's get the driller set up now so we can start first thing," you say.

As Piver and a couple of the others start untying the various parts of the drill from the sledge, Gagnon gives the sky a nervous glance and slides over to you.

"You sure you don't want to set up camp first? If it rains higher up, we won't get much warning. I'd feel a lot happier if we had some extra anchors in and some tarps up."

You shake your head. "No we need to take a few chances if we're going to succeed in this mission."

Gagnon kicks the ground. He doesn't look happy.

You stare him down. This decision isn't up to him. "Now go and show them where to drill and leave the rest up to me."

He shrugs, "Okay, but I don't like it."

Gagnon slides over to where Piver is assembling the drill, pulls out his compass and start taking sightings. Then he plots the exact position where the machine is to be mounted on the slippery black rock. Lengths of pipe are stacked nearby so they can be added to the drill shaft as it bores deeper into the cliff.

Piver and one of the Lowlanders carry over the heavy diamond bit and Piver attaches it to the front of the drilling machine.

"Hope this bit doesn't shatter," Piver says. "The machine will be as useless as a blind pango hunter if it does."

You know how Piver feels. If only the bits weren't so heavy you'd have brought a spare. Unfortunately, no matter how you did the loading calculations, there was no way to carry everything you required and an extra bit.

Piver is busy running pulleys and cables that will drive the driller when rain clouds appear over the ridge behind you. Moments later the first raindrops appear.

This is the worst possible scenario for a troop out on the Black Slopes. Rain is a Highlanders enemy and even with the first few drops you can feel your boot's grip on the smooth black rock starting to go.

"Emergency Anchors! Now!" you yell as you pull the anchor gun from your belt and fire a bolt into the rock at your feet. "Quick! Clip on!"

Full on rain is falling now. Unfortunately some of the others aren't so quick to secure themselves.

To your right, Drexel and Piver have anchored themselves to the now treacherous slope, but some of the Lowlanders aren't so lucky.

When water starts pouring down Black Gully and onto

the plateau, the sledges are in danger of being washed away by the flash flood and you wish you'd got your troop to secure themselves better before worrying about the drill.

Then there is a yell from Piver and you see the supply sledge straining on its single tether. Piver is trying to get across the slope to put an extra anchor in, but he's having problems staying attached to the mountain himself.

A screaming Lowlander goes sliding past, heading for the bottom. Moments later, another trooper is dislodged and lost to the mountain.

With a tortured screech of metal, the supply sledge's anchor bolt is straining. Then with a *ping*, the bolt snaps and the sledge is skidding down the mountain with most of your supplies.

"Geebus!" Piver yells as he struggles to hang on to Shoola, who's slipped down onto him from above. "So much for dinner tonight."

As the water rises, the drilling machine is hit by the torrent and off it slides. The machine misses Trodie by a foot. Trodie is white and shaking, clinging for dear life onto his tether. Thankfully, by sheer strength and determination, Dagma and Drexel have managed to keep the other sledge on the mountain, but only because it's nearly empty.

Then as quickly as it started, the rain stops and the excess water runs away.

Gagnon puts in an extra anchor and then rappels down to your position. "Well, that went well," he says, shaking his head and cursing under his breath.

You look around at the chaos and realize your expedition is over. Why didn't you secure the camp and put in extra anchors for the sledges before you tried to set up the drill? Why didn't you listen to Gagnon? You remember a lecture you had at slider school about the difference between speed and haste.

Haste has cost you two members of your expedition and any self respect you once had. Now you have no option but to struggle back to the Pillars of Haramon with your tail between your legs and beg forgiveness for your lack of judgment.

"Watch out WAVs!" Piver yells.

You whip your head around and look up the slope, but you see no WAV's. "What are you going on about, Piver!" you yell in anger.

"Sorry," Piver says, kicking the ground. "I didn't mean to scare you. I was just trying to show everyone that things could be worse."

And Piver is absolutely right ... but only just.

I'm sorry but this part of your story is over. You've made a bad decision and have lost all your equipment and food and you have to go back to the Pillars of Haramon. However you still have a decision to make. All is not lost. Do you:

Go back to the beginning and start over? **P1**

Or

Go back to your last choice and choose to set up camp? **P57**

You have decided to set up camp first in case the weather turns.

"Let's get camp set up. I saw a hint of clouds earlier, no point in taking any chances," you say. "We need shelter, food and rest."

There are smiles amongst the Highlanders and Lowlanders alike. Everyone's had a long slide and they're hungry. Even those who've ridden on the sledges need to stretch their tired backs and legs.

Piver takes charge of setting up camp. "Tether the sledges with at least three bolts each and put some bolts into the cliff," he says. "Then we can swing some hammocks between the two in case it rains."

After helping to rig up a secure camp the burners are set up in the lee of one of the sledges to get broth heating.

Trodie hands you an energy bar from his home village in the Lowlands. "It's made from crackleberries. Tried them?"

You've tasted crackleberries once before. The thought of the sweet fruit has your mouth watering before you even bite into it. "Yummo," you sigh as a burst of flavor fills your mouth. "Oh, that's soooo good."

Trodie smiles. "It's funny, you Highlanders like crackleberries as much as we Lowlanders love roast pango. I think trade is going to be brisk between us."

"Ummm," you say smacking your lips and licking your fingers. "I'm all for that."

"Here Trodie," you say. "Try one of my snacks, it's from my uncle's hydro pod, he binds the different fungi together with bird fat. If you like roast pango you'll love these."

Before long everyone is sitting around the burners sipping broth and exchanging treats. Dagma has a greasy smile on her face and Piver is jiggling happily as he eats handfuls of dried berries.

You look along the towering cliff as it stretches off into the distance. You can't imagine the force it would have taken to lift such a massive block of rock.

Trodie seems to read your mind. "Feeling small?"

You nod. "Smaller than small really."

"I wonder how many thousands of years ago it all happened," Trodie says. "Imagine being here to witness it."

You turn towards Trodie. "My teachers at school say the Tyron Cliffs were formed long before our species arrived on this planet."

Trodie is about to reply when you hear a distinct rustling sound from above. And it's getting closer!

"WAVs!" you yell. "Hit the deck!"

Grasping your safety line you throw yourself onto the smooth rock behind one of the sledges. Trodie lands beside you just as a huge ball of thorns slams onto the spot where he was sitting.

There is a shower of dust as the rogue WAV bounces off downhill.

"Phew," you say. "That was close."

You pick up one of the thorns left behind by the WAV and examine it. The thorn is an inch and a half long with a barbed point of bright green. You would have expected the thorn to have been brown and dried but this one is different from any you've seen before.

"The tip is still alive," you say, holding it up for Trodie to see. "Look it's moving."

The tip of the thorn is wiggling around as if it's trying to escape. In no time at all, the thorn sprouts a small tendril near its base which wraps itself around your finger. At the end of the tendril, another smaller thorn sprouts.

"Do you believe this?" Trodie asks. "How is it growing so fast?"

"I don't know," you say. "It's not normal for something to grow right in front of your eyes. Even the fastest growing fungi take overnight to grow."

Trodie nods. "Yes, something's very strange."

You have a thought and look over at Trodie. "Imagine if my uncle could cross breed this fast growing plant with edible hydro. Food could grow twice as big in half the time."

"Maybe you should take the plant back with you and

get your uncle to run some trials."

You're about to agree with Trodie when the plant whips its tendril back and then springs forward stabbing your finger and burying its newly grown thorn deep into the flesh of your finger. A drop of green blood runs down your finger and puddles in your palm.

"Ouch!" you yell. "That little beastie just stabbed me!"

You pluck the thorn from your finger and suck on the wound.

"It's growing another tendril," Trodie says, his eyes wide. "And a new thorn!"

Trodie's right. The plant is growing like crazy and is already waving a second thorn about in a threatening manner.

"Yikes," you say, flinging the plant down the slope where it turns itself into a small ball and rolls off. "It's like it could tell I was going to take it with me and attacked! I don't care how fast it grows, I don't want my food crossed with that!"

You and Trodie look around to make sure there aren't any more thorns lying on the ground around the camp

Trodie smiles. "At least crackleberries don't bite."

The first drops of rain come not long after you and the others have climbed into your hammocks. You're thankful you decided to make camp first rather than set up the drill.

Within five minutes, the wind is howling and the rain

is pounding down. Anything not tethered is swept down the mountain. Your sliders lose nothing. They know to clip equipment to their anchored sledges, even when the weather looks good.

The Lowlanders aren't so fortunate. A couple of their supply containers get washed away, much to Trodie's dismay. You remind yourself to keep an eye out for wild pango colonies. You'll need to replace the lost food.

It isn't long before the patter of rain on the waterproof cover above you and the slight swaying of the hammock lulls you to sleep.

By the time you wake up, the sun is creeping over the ridge to the east and the slopes around you are steaming as the remaining moisture evaporates. Within half an hour of the sun hitting the slope, the heat-absorbing rock is dry and burners are warming broth.

Piver is already on the job and has a couple of the Lowlanders carrying equipment to the spot Gagnon has designated for the big drill. The machine is clamped onto metal track bolted onto the slope. A circular shaped blue-diamond drill bit is mounted onto the machine's front spindle while gears and pulleys are attached to the drive unit at the rear. Lengths of pipe to extend the drill's shaft as it bores into the rock are stacked nearby.

Drexel, the expedition's expert climber, brings you a cup of broth and watches the engineers set up ready for drilling. "I bet I could climb this wall in less time than it takes to drill a hole through thirty yards of black glass," he tells you.

With raised eyebrows you look at Drexel. "Really? You're awfully confident." You're surprised at this claim from Drexel. Normally he's not one to brag. "What makes you think that?"

"I was checking out Piver's new hand-held launcher," he says. "Using those and some climbing studs I could free climb it in about four hours I reckon."

You look up at the sheer wall of black glass and then back at a grinning Drexel. "You're crazy. The cliff is straight up."

"At least give me a go. What happens if the drill breaks down halfway through and we've wasted the best part of a day."

Drexel has a point. After losing some of the Lowlander's supplies in the rain, speed is even more critical than before. Maybe Drexel climbing the cliff is your plan B. But then what happens if Drexel falls and you don't have your best climber when it comes time to scale Mount Kakona?

Both options have their risks and rewards.

It is time to make a decision. Do you:

Allow Drexel to climb the Tyron Cliffs? **P113**

Or

Trust that Piver can drill through the cliffs? **P125**

You have decided to go down the watercourse.

"Let's go down the watercourse," you tell Gagnon. "Water always finds the easiest route down a mountain. We may as well follow its trail and do the same."

Gagnon nods his approval and moves out, his sledge tracking along behind him. Two burley sliders have hooked their harnesses to the back of Gagnon's sledge and have their diamond hooks at the ready.

The watercourse is smooth but narrow. This means many zigzagging turns are required to keep the sledges from gaining too much speed as you descend. None the less, Gagnon is an expert guide and it isn't long before a couple of side streams join up and the watercourse becomes wider and more easily negotiated.

You reach the bush line forty-five minutes later. Trees and other strange plants begin to crowd the banks of the watercourse. After an hour, the dried up watercourse is a ribbon of black glass running through a forest of green, the likes of which you've never seen before.

When you see a suitable spot, you signal a halt. "Let's make camp here," you say, pointing to a level patch of moss-covered ground above the watercourse. "There's no black glass so we won't have to watch our step."

Getting off the black glass of the watercourse is a relief. You can't remember the last time you could walk about without worrying if your feet would slide out from under you. To have something so soft underfoot feels like a dream. Normally moss is for eating or used on sleeping platforms. Only the wealthy can afford to buy moss from the Borderlands traders and have it carried into the Highlands.

The sliders anchor the sledges to the bank and start unloading supplies into the clearing. Some of the troopers set up burners while others rig up some basic protection against any rain that might come your way.

When all that is done, you sit around the warmth of a burner and enjoy some steamed fungi, shredded hydro and a cup of hot broth. The sky looks like it's on fire, as the colors of sunset spreads across it.

The jungle is noisier than you expected and many sounds are unfamiliar. Unlike the Lowlanders, you've been brought up on the Black Slopes where the only sounds are the flit of phosphorescent moon moths, or the call of wild pangos. Trees are an alien species to you. Black rock is what you know. Rock and tunnels bored into the mountainside that your communities use for their hydro farms, accommodation pods, schools and markets.

Piver comes and sits beside you. "Geebus it's different down here."

"Tell me about it," you say. "All this greenery makes me nervous.'

"I know what you mean," Piver says, looking left then

right then left again. "Am I being paranoid or is the jungle getting closer?"

You look around. A few of the plant's leaves are quivering slightly, but that is most likely from the slight breeze. In the half-light of late afternoon it's hard to tell exactly where the jungle begins.

"Everything looks okay to—" You stop midsentence when one of the plants on the edge of the clearing reshapes itself into a ball and rolls slowly towards you. "What the...?"

"Geebus!" Piver jumps up. "What is that thing?"

Others around you turn their heads and watch as the ball stops about two yards short of where you are sitting and starts changing shape again.

Then suddenly Piver is doing a nervous jig, hopping from foot to foot in excitement. "Am I going nuts or did that plant just changed itself into a chair?"

You are about to tell Piver to stand back when he rushes over and plonks himself down. "Wow comfy!" he says as the chair adjusts to fit his body shape. "All it needs is a footstool."

There is a collective 'oooohhhh' as the front part of the bush reforms into a footrest.

Another ball of green rolls up, this one reforms into a long couch. Two troopers rush over and sit down. Then another ball comes, and another.

Before long your whole troop is lounging in comfort,

laughing and drinking broth.

You wonder if this is such a good idea. If these plants are reforming into things at the request of your sliders, it means they are thinking. What's to say they will remain friendly? What if someone scares or annoys one of these remarkable creatures.

Still, the plants seem harmless … eager to please even.

You squat next to one of the green balls. "Can you hear me?"

The ball of green turns into an animal shape, small, four legs, a tail that wags. It jumps up on your lap and a small tendril tickles your face.

"Stop it," you giggle, pulling your face back.

The animal sits back on its haunches and lifts both front legs. It turns its head from side to side, as if it's looking at you, or waiting for a command.

"Can you reform into anything?" you ask the creature.

The animals shakes its head.

"But you understand what I'm saying?"

The animal nods and leaps up to tickle your face again.

"We are looking for tyranium crystal. Do you know what those are?"

The animal shakes its head and turns into a chair. You smile and take a seat. As soon as you're comfortable, vines wrap around your wrists and ankles.

"What are you doing?" you ask the plant. "Dagma! Piver!" you yell unable to move your limbs. When you turn your head you see that everyone is tied up. The plants have captured your entire expedition.

"We mean you no harm," you plead. "Why are you doing this?"

A large half man half plant walks out of the jungle. "I see you've met my pets."

You pull as hard as you can, but as you do, the vines around your wrists squeeze tighter. You look up at the strange man-plant. "Why are you doing this? We mean you know harm."

"Invaders always say that. Then the next thing you know they are chopping down the trees and digging up the ground."

"But we're just looking for tyranium needle crystal," you say. "We're happy to trade for them."

More plants close in on your group. Some of them block off your retreat and form a wall of interlaced branches that surrounds you like a cage.

The man-plant reforms into a larger animal, with a single horn in the middle of its forehead and long fangs. "We don't need your trinkets," the beast growls. "We get what we need from the soil and the rain and each other. History tells us this is all we need."

"History?" you ask. "What history is that and why didn't I learn about it in school?"

"It is the history of the planet our ancestors came from, that your ancestors came from," the beast says.

"The desire for more and more ruined that planet."

"But you're—you're not... Petronian. You're half—"

"—plant. Yes. Some DNA splicing was done on the long journey it took us to get here from our home planet, your home planet. We are now the best of both species."

You wonder if this creature is related to those thorny tumbleweeds that grow on your side of the mountains. "So are all the plants on Petron related?"

"More than you'll ever realize."

This is all very fascinating, but you wonder why he's giving you so much information. Unless he knows you'll never have a chance to...

"Get some sleep," the man-plant says. "We move to our settlement by the lake in the morning. We can talk more once we're there." And with that, the creature steps back and transforms into part of the cage that now completely surrounds you.

The plants release your arms and legs. You stand rubbing your wrists and stretch while looking at the impenetrable wall around you. Others do the same. You need to talk to Gagnon and Piver about this development and make some sort of plan. But how do you do this without these creatures hearing you?

As the last of the light goes, the plants go still.

As you make your way towards where Piver is standing, Dagma grabs your sleeve.

"I have moth mist," she says sheepishly.

You raise a finger to your lips and shake your head slightly. You instantly understand what Dagma is suggesting. You also know she is risking severe disciplinary action for bringing a prohibited substance along on the expedition.

Moth mist, is a potent chemical compound collected from the moon moths that inhabit the Highlands. When inhaled, the mist gives one an intense feeling of tranquility. Some sliders use it to help them sleep.

"It we spray the plants we might be able to escape while they're dreaming," Dagma says.

You're unsure. Reactions to chemicals are never guaranteed and plants and animals have different nervous systems. What if the mist has the opposite reaction to plants as it has to people and makes them agitated?

It is time to make a decision. Do you:

Spray the plants with moth mist and try to escape? **P77** Or

Wait until tomorrow and see what happens? **P80**

You have decided to go west and zigzag down the broad ridge.

"I like the idea of being able to see what's coming," you say. "Let's take the ridge. It's good sliding rock all the way to the valley floor, and we won't need to offload the sledges and carry our supplies through the jungle like we would if the streambed is blocked."

Gagnon takes another look at the ridge through his scope. "I agree. It's going to be technical at the top but it gets wider and easier further down. The jungle's growing right to the rock's edge, but that shouldn't create any problems."

Your troop is quick to reorganize from climbing mode to sliding mode. Dagma takes the brake position at the back of the first sledge. Once everyone is ready Gagnon leads offs.

It's a short traverse to the top of the ridge. Then, in a series of tight S-turns, your little caravan weaves it way down the narrow band of rock. About forty minutes and 2000 feet of altitude later, you see a level area off to the right with an enormous overhang that will give your group some protection from the elements.

You signal a halt. "Let's camp over there for the night," you tell the group. "It never hurts to have some natural protection from the rain."

The exhausted group is quick to agree. They break out

the windbreaks and sling their hammocks between the sledges and the rock wall. Others set up burners and get some broth heating.

Villum sits and watches as the others set up the camp.

"Where are some roosting pangos when you need them," Piver says in passing.

You smile. "Just go make friends with him. Remember, your job is to learn everything about that step cutting machine."

Piver does as he's told while other sliders distribute hot broth and dehydrated fungi.

You look at the landscape below. Towards the volcano's crater, as the last of the light glistens off its shimmering black slopes, you wonder if it's cloud, steam or smoke that you see. Then you notice a red glow along the volcano's southern flank.

"Hey Gagnon," you say. "Come have a look at this."

Gagnon slides over and pulls out his scope. "An active vent by the looks of it. Could make things tricky if there's poison gas about."

"How will we know?" you asks.

"It's not easy. Hydrogen sulfide is heavier than air and can flow down the mountainside like an invisible wave. You don't know it's there until you take your last deadly breath."

"Just what we need."

"There is a solution though," Gagnon says. "If we can

catch a few pango and keep them in cages, they can warn us of the presence of poisonous gas."

You remember hearing about this technique but you're not sure you remember the details. "Is it because the pangos are more sensitive than we are?"

Gagnon nods. "Yip. The pangos fall over at about three parts per million. We can take about 30 before we pass out."

"So, as soon as a pango hits the bottom of the cage, we get sliding."

"And quickly," Gagnon says. "We won't have much time."

You ponder what Gagnon's said as you sip your broth. Where are you going to find wild pango on this side of the divide? And how are you going to catch them even if you do?

"Hey Dagma," you say pulling her away from her meal of hydro. "You didn't happen to see any pangos this side of the pass did you?"

You know Dagma hunts pango with other members of her family when she's not transporting people around the Black Slopes as part of the Slider Corps. You also know she's got a keen eye for the Highland delicacy.

Dagma ponders a moment. "I heard a small group nesting on a pinnacle about 500 feet further up and out to the east."

"Do you think you could catch them?"

"If I had a net launcher I could but…"

"Piver's got a new handheld cable launcher. Maybe he could adapt it?"

Dagma smiles. "Yeah he mentioned that. I'll go find out."

Dagma's back a few minutes later with good news. "He's going to work on it tonight. I'll climb back up at first light and see if they're still there. How many do you want?"

"Just a couple should do," you say. "Any extras you can cook up."

"Yummo," Dagma says, licking her lips. "I love pango."

After a restless night dreaming of volcanoes, dawn breaks clear and warm. As the camp starts to wake, you see the silhouette of Dagma climbing back up the ridge She carries a cage made of fine mesh stretched over a lightweight frame. It will be an hour at least before she returns so you get together with Gagnon and start planning your route to the volcano.

In his role as chief spy and information gatherer, Piver has taken on the role of servant to Villum and takes him some broth and a bowl of hydro. You can hear Piver flattering Villum about his expert operation of the step cutter.

Villum strokes his own ego by telling Piver about the machine's construction and operation. "What makes my machine so good," Villum says, puffing out his chest, "is the hammer mechanism built into its base. It gives the drill extra punch when penetrating the rock."

"Oh how interesting," Piver says, grinning at the bragging Lowlander. "You are so clever, Villum. Tell me more."

Meanwhile, after studying the terrain further, you and Gagnon decide to follow the ridge all the way to the valley floor and then unpack what vital equipment you'll need to mine the tyranium and transport it by foot to the base of the volcano.

"Let's just hope we can find this canyon," you say. "Otherwise we'll have to climb the volcano and look around the vents higher up."

"Not a pleasant thought," Gagnon says. "That's like climbing an explosion waiting to happen."

Gagnon's comment sends a shiver down your spine. He's not wrong. Everywhere you look around Petron you see evidence of its violent and explosive past.

You are about to send a search party out for Dagma when you hear a 'woot woot' from above. As she nears, you see she's managed to net four pango.

"Two for you," Dagma says with a smile. "And two for me. Nom, nom."

"Well done. Now let's harness up and get ready to move," you say. "We've got a fair bit of rock to cover today."

Once again Gagnon and his sledge take the lead. The going gets easier with every foot of altitude you lose. But then strange holes begin to appear in the surface and Gagnon is forced to take evasive action.

You signal a halt and get everyone to tether their sledges. "These holes don't look natural," you say. "Far too regular to be lava tubes formed during an eruption."

"Hey Piver," you say, "get over here and tell me what you think."

After a bit of fiddling about, Piver attaches a cable to a sledge and lowers himself to the edge of one of the holes. "Looks like it's been made by machine," Piver says. "I see drill marks and it goes down at a nice uniform angle. I wonder where they lead?"

"Could they have been made by people living on this side of the mountain range?" you ask.

"Either that or aliens," Piver says with a grin.

So what are the odds? you think. Did someone come from a distant part of the universe just to drill holes in the side of a mountain and then disappear, or were they made by someone living here?

"I think we need to double our lookout," you say to the troop. "The odds tell me someone's living on this side of the mountain."

"Maybe we should investigate and see where they lead," Villum says.

"Great idea LoLa!" Dagma says in a sarcastic tone.

"You go first. I'll give you a hand over the edge."

Villum pretends to tighten his boots, ignoring Dagma's comment.

You look at Piver. "Is it possible they're transport tunnels or perform some other function?"

"It's possible they go all the way through the planet and end up on the other side of the ocean in a land of twinkling stars and purple monsters, but I somehow doubt it. More likely they've been drilled by the locals looking for something. Water collectors maybe? Impressive technology if that's the case."

Piver doesn't seem too sure. You like the idea of them being transport tunnels to a settlement further down the mountain, but perhaps Piver's right.

It is time to make a decision. Do you:

Send someone down the hole to investigate? **P86**

Or

Carry on down the ridge? **P98**

You have decided to spray the plants with moth mist and try to escape.

"Dagma," you whisper. "How much mist have you got? Do you think there's enough to spray all the plants?"

Dagma's face goes red. "I've got quite a bit. It's the only way I can get to sleep these days." From a pocket in her tunic, she pulls out a bottle, three quarters full of a bright blue liquid and hands it to you.

"We can't slide in the dark so we'll have to make a break at first light," you say, tucking the bottle of mist into your pocket. "In the mean time, let's tell the others what's happening, but do it quietly. We can't let our captors to find out what we're planning."

Dagma nods and moves off to spread the word. You do the same.

It isn't long before everyone is in on the plan and settles down to catch a few hours sleep and wait for first light.

Your internal clock wakes you as Petron's largest moon rises above the horizon. You can tell from its angle that sunrise is not far away. Secreting the bottle of moth mist in your sleeve, you get up and walk to the wall of plants.

The plunger on the bottle shoots a fine mist out of its nozzle and coats the nearest leaf. You make your way around the wall of green giving it a burst every few feet.

Then you step back and wait.

Nothing happen for the first few minutes, but then there's a slight slumping of the rigid framework the plants have formed around you. Within five minutes the vines are unraveling like crazy and slipping to the ground.

You walk to the wall and force your hands between some of the branches and push them apart. They feel rubbery, like they've lost all their strength.

"I think they're asleep," you say to the troop. "Let's get loaded and get out of here."

Things go well until the first ray of sunlight comes over the ridge. As soon as it hits the leaves, the plants spring back to life. Some of them start weaving around your legs and arms. One wraps itself around your neck.

Before you can do anything, everyone is trussed up and unable to move.

When you look around you see the man-plant again. He is angry and has formed his bulk into a large tooth-filled mouth. A strong tendril wraps around one of your troopers, lifts him off the ground and tosses him into the gaping maw.

Moments later the plant burps and spits out a pile of bones.

"Yum, tasty," the huge mouth says. "I was going to take you back to our community and see if we could come to some peaceful arrangement, but you have proven yourselves untrustworthy. Looks like you'll have to be breakfast instead."

And with that the tendril tightens around your neck and your vision goes black.

I'm sorry, but this part of your story is over. You decided to drug your captors and try to escape. That made them angry and they've eaten you for breakfast. Burp!

However all is not lost. You still have three possible choices. Do you:

Go back to your last decision and choose to wait until morning rather than drugging your captors? **P80**

Or

Go back to the beginning of the story and try another path? P1

Or

Go to the list of choices and start reading from another part of the story? **P204**

You have decided to wait and see what happens tomorrow.

You decide it's not worth the risk of trying to drug the plants. They might change into something dangerous and then the whole expedition would be in danger.

"Let's try talking first," you tell Dagma. "If we can get them to trust us, who knows what benefits that could bring. You call Piver, Gagnon and Villum over and tell them your decision."

"Okay," Dagma says, turning to go to her sleeping position.

"Wait," you say, putting your hand out. "Aren't you forgetting something?"

Dagma shrugs, delves into her pocket and comes out with a bottle of bright blue liquid.

You stretch your hand out a little more and Dagma reluctantly puts the bottle into your hand.

"You can breathe in all the mist you like in your own time Dagma, but when you're on patrol, and others are counting on you, it's just not on. Now, get back to the others and try to get some sleep. Tomorrow I want you bright and ready."

If the situation were different, you would have punished Dagma and have her standing guard duty all night, but you suspect losing her mist is enough and you want her fresh in the morning.

Villum isn't happy. "I'd rather escape. I don't trust these—these animals."

"Tough," you say. "I'm in charge so be smart and keep your mouth shut. Diplomacy is the key right now."

The next morning as the sun rises over the ridge, your troopers start stirring. You can hear the rustling of leaves as the plants reform themselves into balls in preparation for the trip to the lake.

The man-plant is back in the form of a person and steps forward to talk to you. "If you try to run, or harm any of my pets you will be caught and eaten. But if you are trustworthy I will guarantee your safety."

You gulp and nod your head. "Okay, we'll play nice."

"Good. I suggest you climb aboard your sledges. My pets will escort you through the jungle."

You're not sure what the man-plant has in mind, but you instruct your sliders to climb aboard.

Villum has other ideas. He marches up to the man-plant and puts his hands on his hips. "I demand some respect here," he says to the plant. "My father is a general and if you don't—"

Faster than you can imagine, the plant turns into a snake and wraps its body around Villum's body and starts squeezing. "How about a hug? Would you like one of those you arrogant fool?"

Villum grunts, his eyes bulging. When he's about as blue as the moth mist you confiscated from Dagma, the plant releases him and reforms back into the shape of a person.

"Care to climb aboard now young general's son? Or would you like another hug?"

Villum, still gasping for air, wastes no time in climbing aboard the nearest sledge.

You're amazed by the power of these creatures, but also impressed at how quickly they've put the demanding Villum in his place. They might become quite an ally after all.

Once everyone is aboard a sledge the plants reform around them, lift them off the ground and roll away down the watercourse towards the lake. The plants are much faster downhill than traveling by sledge would have been. Before much more than an hour has passed, your convoy is rolling up to a strange structure with metallic feathers covering its surface. Beyond this structure is a beautiful lake. The plants put down your sledges and the next thing you know, tiny metal birds are flitting around you, probing with their tiny beaks and looking at you with their telescopic eyes.

"These must be some of the robots that crazy old miner was talking about," you tell Piver who is staring, fascinated by the creatures. "Or maybe I should say, the not so crazy miner, as it turns out."

A circular door in the side of the structure opens and a number of people come out. They look at you like you're some sort of curiosity.

"Welcome to New Londinium," the oldest woman of the group says. "I see you've met Eva and her little friends."

You climb down off your sledge and smile in greeting. "We come in friendship seeking trade with your people."

The woman smiles. "I doubt you've much to offer that we don't have already."

You are thankful that Villum has learned his lesson and sits quietly. Piver is curious. He jumps down and comes to stand beside you.

"You sure about that?" Piver says, holding up a cold leg of deep fried pango.

"What is that?" the woman asks.

"Here, taste." Piver steps forward and passes the woman the pango leg.

The woman sniffs and then tastes a tiny bit, weary of some trick.

"Geebus, lady, just bite right in. It's the tastiest thing in the whole world. ... apart from crackleberries maybe."

The woman's next bite is a little larger. As she chews, her eyes brighten. She smiles at Piver. "What is this delicious morsel? Such flavor, so—so succulent!"

Piver smiles back and does a little jig. "Pango, pango, pango, pango ... Leg of pango is my favorite. It's the taste that makes me happy. Pango, pango, pango pang," he sings.

"And you can get more of this?" the woman asks.

"Much as you'd like," Piver says. "My dad's a pango hunter. The eggs are pretty good too."

You clear your throat and look at the woman. "We just need a few tyranium crystals in exchange. It's a win-win don't you think?"

The woman takes another bite of pango and then licks her fingers. "You've got a deal … on one condition."

You nod. "Sure if we can. What is it?"

"We have lots of tyranium, but we need to cement our new relationship with a wedding. My eldest daughter is of marriageable age and needs a husband. After an unusual run of girl children, we've very few men left in our community."

This is not what you expected. "Well sure, I guess. Who did you have in mind?"

The woman turns and waves her daughter forward. "I think it is for her to decide, don't you?"

"Sure, I suppose," you say.

"Geebus," Piver whispers. "She's beautiful."

"She is also our genetic engineering specialist," the woman says.

The tyranium trade is vital to your communities. If a marriage will seal the deal then that's what you'll do. "Okay," you say. "As long as whoever your daughter selects agrees as well. It's only fair."

"Agreed." The woman turns to her daughter. "What

do you think darling? See anyone you like?"

"I could give your daughter a good life," Villum says, stepping forward. He give the girl a quick once over, smiling at what he sees. "I'm the son of a general and have many servants. I could give your daughter a life of luxury."

The girls looks at Villum. "But what work do you do? What knowledge do you have?"

Villum is a bit dumbstruck at her question. "But I have riches, and farmlands, and—"

The girl smiles and reaches out her arm. The arm turns into a long slim tendril and wraps itself around Piver's hand. "But I like this one," the girl says. "He's funny, and clever and smells of pango."

Piver smiles. As he steps forward he does a happy little jiggle. "Me? Really? Geebus! I'd be honored."

Congratulations you have finished this part of the story. You have found not only a new source of tyranium crystals essential to your communities, but you found another tribe living on Petron. But have you tried all the different paths this story has?

It is time to make another decision. Do you:

Go back to the beginning and try another path? **P1**

Or

Go to the list of choices and read from somewhere else in the story? **P204**

You have decided to send someone down the hole to investigate.

"I think we should investigate. These holes could give us a clue to the people living on this side of the range."

"Or get us killed," Piver says a little nervously. "I volunteer to stay here."

"I'll go," Dagma says. "Anything if it means we don't have to lug our gear through the jungle."

You clip a zip line onto a sledge and carefully lower yourself to the edge of the hole. When you look down into it you see tiny dots of light attached to the smooth rock. "Moon moths have taken up residence," you say. "How much cable have we got, Piver?"

"A mile maybe, if we join it all together. You're not serious about going down there?"

"If moon moths are living here, how dangerous can it be?"

"Moon moths are insects, how smart do you think they are?" Piver asks.

The little engineer has a point. Moon moths aren't the cleverest of creatures, but then again, you've never see them nest in areas of danger so you have trust their instincts.

You look at Piver. "Get out the cable and a winch. I'm going in."

"Geebus! You're crazy." Piver shakes his head and

zips back up to the sledge. He sets about rigging up a winch, splicing some cables together and feeding it onto the drum. About fifteen minutes later he tosses you a line.

"Here you go. What signal are you going to use when you want us to pull you back up? A blood-curdling scream?"

You give him a stern look. "Not funny, Piver."

Piver hands you one of his new hand held launchers. "Okay, fire this when you've had enough. I've detached the tether so we'll see the line when it comes shooting out of the hole."

"You sure you don't want me to go?" Dagma says.

You shake your head. "I'll be fine."

Piver stands by the winch and releases the break. "Right you're in control. Good luck."

After double checking that the cable is properly attached to your harness, you lean back, let out some cable, and step into space. With your feet apart for balance, you start the long slide down the tunnel.

At first there is light radiating from the luminescent wings of the moon moths to give you an idea of the dimensions of the tunnel, but it isn't long before you've left them behind and are sliding in total darkness. It's an eerie feeling and you find yourself unable to tell how fast you're going apart from the hum of the cable running though the clip on your harness.

Then you see a strange glow below you ... and it's getting brighter.

You slow the release of cable and proceed with more caution. When the tunnel widens out, you find yourself in an old lava tube filled with enormous crystals. The pale blue light they emit gives the tunnel an eerie glow and just enough light for you to see the extent of the crystal field. Some crystal are bigger than tree trunks and it's hard to believe you're not dreaming.

Using the diamond studs on the heels your boots, you work your way over to a flat section where you can stand up and loop a length of cable around one of the smaller crystals.

You can't believe the size and number of crystals down here. There's no tyranium needle crystals unfortunately, but these diamonds more than make up for their absence.

Then further into the old lave tube, you see the teeth of what you suspect is a drilling tool of some sort, lying to one side. It's similar to the drills that the Highlanders use for boring accommodation pods and hydro growing chambers but this one is huge and has red teeth made from a material you've not seen before. Whoever developed this monster has technology that far surpasses what the Highlanders or Lowlanders have. And that makes you a little nervous.

After another look around, you pull Piver's handheld

launcher out of your utility belt, aim it up the tunnel and pull the trigger.

With a hiss of compressed air, the bolt shoots up trailing twenty yards of filament behind it. Now it's just a matter of waiting to be winched to the surface.

When Piver sees the bolt shoot into the sky, he flips the switch on the winch. "Okay everyone, here we go."

The winch starts to turn and slowly the cable wraps around the drum.

You and the eight-foot-long crystal slowly rise up the tunnel. Soon you're seeing pinpoints of light from the moon moths again and then, as you near the surface, a disk of sunlight appears.

When you and the crystal emerge from the top of the hole, everyone looks on in amazement.

"Geebus!" Piver says. "What is that thing?"

Gagnon slides over for a closer look. "I think it's the largest blue diamond ever discovered."

"Wrong," you say, not quite believing what you're about to say. "There are others down there that are ten times bigger!"

Gagnon's eyes pop. "How is that even possible?"

"I don't know but it's true. And … there's a huge drill bit down there too, so…"

"We're not alone," Gagnon says.

"No. And they may not like us finding their mine."

This gives everyone something to consider. A few on

the expedition have lost their smiles and are looking around as if they're expecting an attack at any moment.

You are still marveling at your discovery when you see an unusual metallic bird hovering nearby. Then you hear the sound of metal scraping on rock and see a metal spider skittering across the rock towards you. The spider's body is round and has a number of cogs on it. Its eight legs are equipped with miniature drills on their tips that help it attach itself to the slippery rock as it moves.

"Looks like that miner wasn't so nutty after all," you say to the others. "Look! Spiderbot."

Then you hear a voice coming from the spider. "Attention, newcomers. Please do not fear."

Piver's jaw drops. "Is that—is that thing talking to us?"

You look at the spider and then at the bird. Then you realize the bird is made of metal too and has delicate silver feathers. Its eyes are made of clear glass and they rotate and move in and out as the bird stares at you.

You take a step towards the spider. "Can you hear me?"

"Yes, newcomers, we can hear you."

"Geebus!" Piver says, peering down at the robot. "This is incredible."

"We mean you no harm," the voice coming from the spider says. "Do not fear."

Silently your sliders have moved into a defensive

formation around the spider. Their guide sticks and slingshots at the ready.

"Easy," you say to your troop. "Let's hear the machine out."

The spider skitters a little closer. "Follow the spiderbot and it will bring you safely to us. Leave the diamond crystal, you will be permitted to take it with you when you return to your people."

You move closer to Gagnon. "What do you think?" you whisper. "They sound friendly enough."

"Looks like their technology's superior to ours. We'd better do as they say."

You look at the spiderbot and then the metallic bird. "Okay, we will follow as you ask. We come in peace and are only in search of minerals."

Without another word, the spider scurries over to the edge of the ridge where the smooth black rock meets the softer soil and foliage of the jungle. "Please tether your sledges and then come this way," it says. "We have a means of transportation over here."

Directing your troops to do as the spider says, you follow the spiderbot to where a metal snake, fifteen yards long and eight feet round, sits waiting. The snake is made from flexible segments and has a drill bit, similar to the one you saw underground, attached to its front end. A hatch on the side of the snake opens revealing rows of seats inside.

"Please climb aboard," the spider says.

"Wow," Piver says. "I want one of these!"

You're not surprised that Piver finds this new contraption fascinating. It is a marvel of engineering. Inside the snake, behind the rows of seats is the drive unit. In the front, behind a row of instruments, sits a humanoid shaped robot with funny looking goggles on. Then you realize the goggles are like the hummingbots eyes and are probably relaying what the robot is seeing to a control post somewhere else.

Typically, Piver, in his enthusiasm, is first aboard. You and the other sliders follow. Villum's knees are shaking as he climbs aboard and takes a seat near the back. Then a whirring sound starts and the door closes, locking you and your group inside.

The snake slithers off downhill for a short distance and then dives into a hole. Everything around you goes dark except for the blinking lights of the instrument panel at the front of the snake.

You turn to Gagnon sitting in the next seat. "I hope this isn't a mistake."

Gagnon's skin is a little pale. "You're not the only one."

The underground journey takes less than an hour. When the snake resurfaces and the door reopens, there are a number of buildings built around a much larger structure the likes of which you've never seen. This large structure is bird-shaped and covered in beautiful metallic feathers, similar to those that cover the smaller hummingbot, only larger.

A crowd of people are going about their normal business. Some of them ride on small contraptions that float just off the ground. Others ride on strange beasts that look to be half plant and half animal. The people look like members of your own community only a little greener, thinner and with less muscular legs.

"Please disembark," the spiderbot says as it skitters out.

"What is that thing?" Piver says, pointing to the large structure covered in metal feathers. "I'm sure I've seen a picture of something similar in the *Book of Myths.*"

"I've seen it too," Gagnon says. "It's the part of the myth about how our ancestors arrived on this planet. '*...and they arrived in a giant bird that travelled between the stars,*' it says if I remember correctly."

"Between the stars?" you ask. "You mean from beyond our sun and moons?"

Gagnon smiles. "So the story goes. Looks like the myths are true after all."

"But how would it be possible to travel such distances?" you ask.

"Just because we don't understand how such things happen doesn't mean that it can't. There are many things we will never know."

"But that doesn't mean every crazy idea is possible either," you say, trying to get your head around all this new information."

"But there's lots of things to discover," Piver says. "I learn new stuff every day. That's what makes life so much fun."

As you ponder what your friends have said, a circular door on the side of the structure opens and a ramp lowers to the ground. A group of people, both men and women, old and young, come walking down the ramp towards you.

"Welcome newcomers," a slender, older woman says. "My name is Margaret, Chief Council of Settlement Three."

Margaret reminds you a little of your mother. Her skin is translucent and her face serene. She has laughter lines around her eyes and her expression is open. Most reassuring of all, none of the people carry weapons.

You tuck your guide stick under your arm, take a step forward and bow. "Greetings. I am the leader of our expedition. We come in peace seeking tyranium and blue diamond to help build our settlements on the far side of the mountains."

"Yes, we know. Our hummingbots have been watching your journey ever since you left the Pillars of Haramon," Margaret says. "We have been most pleased that the Highlanders and Lowlanders have found peace.

We would never have allowed you over the pass if you were still in conflict."

Your instincts tell you that these are good people and your tight shoulders begin to relax. You place a hand on your chest below the single diamond pinned there. "I am tasked with finding a new source of tyranium. Is it possible that we could sit down and talk about opening up trade between our people? I'm sure that we have things that would be of benefit to your people too."

"There is one thing we lack on this side of the mountains. Our supply of protein is limited. Unlike yours, our terrain is not very suitable for pangos to breed, so the colonies on this side of the mountains are small. We lack the high pinnacles the birds favor and are reliant on what we can grow in the soil, weak as it is. The snake you rode here is used for terraforming and mining. It turns rock into soil, but the nutrients this soil contains are few."

Dagma steps forward and holds up a cage with four pango in it. "Here are some birds I netted early this morning, before we broke camp. Please take them as a gift."

"Four pangos are a rare treat this side of the mountains. Thank you," the woman says.

"Highlanders catch thousands of pangos each season," you say. "I'm sure we can spare some in exchange for minerals. We could also allow you to mine the rock under the pango colonies with your snake. The phosphate there is the perfect nutrient for growing plants."

Margaret waves you into the structure. "Come, we have much to discuss. In the meantime, take a look around our ship. After all it contains much of your history too."

"Our history?" you ask.

"Yes. The book you call the *Book of Myths* is history not fable. We come from common stock that left our home planet many years ago. During the trip our DNA was improved by crossbreeding it with plants. Our home planet was far richer in oxygen than Petron."

Margaret sees that you are doubtful. She smiles and holds out her hand. You can see the blood vessels through her fine translucent skin. "Do we not all bleed green?"

You have to admit that if her people came from the stars, and you and she are the same, then maybe your people did too. But how did your history get lost over the years?

As if reading your mind Margaret smiles. "We've kept the pass over the mountains closed for generations, waiting for your people to tire of fighting. Much of your historic relics and books were lost during endless conflict. When we found out about the truce and felt it might last, we sent a scout, disguised as a miner, over to your people knowing that you would come for the minerals. Now perhaps we can join together and make Petron better than Earth ever was."

"Earth?" you say. "That's where we originated?"

"Yes, Earth. In the Milky Way Galaxy."

"Geebus!" Piver says. "What a funny name for a planet."

Congratulations, this part of your story has ended. You've led a successful mission to the far side of the mountains and established friendly contact with the people there. The future looks bright.

But have you followed all the paths this story takes?

It is time to make another decision. Do you:

Go back to the beginning and try another path? **P1**

Or

Go to the list of choices and start reading from somewhere else in the story? **P204**

You have decided to carry on down the ridge.

"Let's keep going," you say. "If we have time we can check out these holes on the way back."

Gagnon moves off with his sledge, keeping an extra close eye out for more holes.

As your group loses altitude the ridge keeps broadening out. The stumpy shrubs of the upper mountain are left behind and the jungle gets thicker and taller and closer to the rock you're sliding on. In places, branches overhand the ridge. Some trees tower so high you can't see their tops, while other have a host of smaller plants living in the crooks of their branches.

You're glad the rocky ridge is here. It forms a broad highway running through the dense jungle. It would have been hard trying to find your way through this near impenetrable tangle of vines and creepers.

"I smell fart," Gagnon says as he brings his sledge to a halt.

"It's probably gas from the volcano," Piver says.

"The pangos are still alive so it can't be deadly," Dagma says, holding up the cage with the four birds in it.

A few of the sliders are laughing and blaming each other for the stink. One has her hand at her throat and is doing a good impression of someone choking to death. As Gagnon continues on, the smell gets stronger and stronger until a few expedition members pull the front of their uniforms up over their noses.

"Geebus!" Piver says. "This smells worse than a morph rat hole!"

He's right. You've come across a few rat holes in your day but this stench beats that by a mile. Thankfully, your senses adjust quickly and after another half hour down the ridge you hardly notice it.

Then you hear a loud screech of diamond hooks as Gagnon and his sledge come to an emergency stop.

"Wow, look at that," he calls out.

After your sledge has stopped, you slide forward to Gagnon's position. Below you is a chasm so deep and so beautiful it's hard to believe it's real.

"It must be a half a mile deep," you say.

The multicolored layers of rock change from the darkest black to a pale blue as they go down deeper into the canyon. At the bottom, small craters bubble with magma.

"This has got to be Crater Canyon," Gagnon says.

"That looks like crystal bearing rock near the bottom," Piver says, scanning the canyon through his scope, . "That band of light blue rock is a dead giveaway. Getting to it might be a problem though."

"How much cable have we got?" you ask Piver. "Enough to get us down that far?"

"Sure," Piver says. "We've got lots of cable, but that's not the problem, it's getting the crystals back up again that I'm worried about. Any idea how much half a mile of quarter inch cable weighs?"

"Five feet per pound?" you guess, trying to remember what you learned in slider school.

"Pretty close," Piver says. "So half a mile of cable weighs in at 250 pounds, plus whatever it's attached to. Our winches are only rated to 300 so by the time you add a basket and crystals, they'll be overloaded and burn out."

You rest your guide stick on the ground and look at Piver. "So what do we do?"

"Now that's where an engineer comes in handy," he says. "We'll winch in two stages. We need to lower a team down halfway where they'll construct a platform. From there we can mount another winch that will reach the bottom. That way the cable weight is only 125 pounds max."

You see what the little engineer is getting at. "And we do the reverse on the way back out?"

"No stink on you," he says with a grin. "Apart from that whiff of volcano I smell."

You look up to the sky to make sure there is no sign of rain. Rain would make the ground too slippery to work, even for a slider wearing diamond studded boots. Satisfied the weather will hold, you get Piver and the other engineers to work.

They unload equipment from the sledges and start constructing a sturdy framework complete with brackets so they can bolt it to the canyon wall. Another engineer sets up a winch and bolts it to solid rock.

"Double check your safety lines. I don't want any accidents," you tell your crew.

It's an hour before the newly constructed platform is eased over the edge and two engineers, their belts loaded with equipment climb aboard. Piver takes control of the top winch while another engineer acts as spotter.

You hear the hum of the motor as the winch lowers the platform and the two engineers down the smooth canyon wall. When the desired level is reached, Piver puts on the brake and the engineers start drilling holes in the cliff face and begin attaching the platform with sturdy anchor bolts.

Once the platform is secured to the canyon wall, another winch is lowered. This winch is then mounted onto the platform. Only then can the miners lower themselves to the canyon floor and start looking for the rare crystals you've come so far to find.

After relaying two more miners down the cliff, Piver comes over to you. "I thought I'd go down and have a look."

"Is that a good idea?" you ask. "What if we have problems with the winch?"

"Drexel can look after things up here," Piver says. "Why don't you leave Gagnon in charge and come down too? You've got to admit it's an amazing place. Don't you want to have a look?"

Piver is right. Crater Canyon is an amazing place and Gagnon is a responsible second in command. When are you likely to pass this way again?

But do you want to be so far from the rest of your troop, especially in unknown territory? What if something unexpected happens?

It is time to make a decision. Do you:

Go with Piver into the canyon? **P103**

Or

Stay at the top of the canyon? **P107**

You have decided to go with Piver into the canyon.

"Why not?" you say to Piver. "I'd love to have a closer look."

Piver does an excited hop and rubs his hands together. "Okay, I'll tell Drexel to get ready to drop us down. Grab whatever you need and meet me at the edge."

After sorting out a few supplies you slide to the edge and wait for Piver.

A moment later he arrives with one end of a cable. "Here you go, clip on and get ready to lose your breakfast. It's going to be a scary ride."

You clip your harness onto the cable and lean back testing your weight. Piver does the same.

"Okay now we just have to walk backwards off the cliff and try not to poop ourselves," he says with a cheeky grin. "You ready?"

You take a deep breath. "Let's do it."

Piver waves his arm at Drexel and soon you feel movement in the cable. When you reach the edge you lean back and step over the edge.

"Keep your waist bent and your feet against the rock wall so you don't swing about," Piver says. "And try to enjoy the view."

You have to admit the view is spectacular. The canyon extends for miles in both directions. Internal forces have ripped the ground apart exposing layer upon layer of rock. Far to the east the canyon is filled with a pink mist that has settled near its bottom.

"Okay feet down," Piver says. "Platform coming up."

Once safely on the platform you re-clip your harness to the cable attached to the platform winch. A young miner smiles and lowers you and Piver down the next section. Ten minutes later you are standing at the bottom of Crater Canyon.

"Geebus," Piver says. "It's hot down here."

The little engineer is right. You can feel the sweat trickling down the back of your uniform. Off to your left a couple of the miners have stripped down to their vests in an attempt to stay cool while they drill away at the band of tyranium crystal in the canyon wall. A mound of crystal bearing rock is piled up to one side.

"Looks like rich pickings," you say. "As long as one of these vents don't blow."

Piver looks over at the nearest bubbling pool of magma. "Don't worry, if it erupts you'll never feel a thing."

"That's what I'm afraid of."

Despite the canyon floor being hot and dangerous, it is also a place of great beauty. Everywhere you look the rock is sparkling with crystals of some sort. The miners are laughing as they work, amazed at the size and length of the needle crystals they're finding. But a rumble beneath your feet reminds you how dangerous this place is. "Let's start getting some of this rock back up. We don't want to be down here any longer than we have to," you say to the miners.

"A least the pangos are still kicking," Piver says pointing to a cage near the miners. "No gas at least."

You give Piver a thumbs up. "So far so good."

As the miners load rock into a basket and start winching it back up to the canyon rim, you look around at the different strata of rock. One layer is made of tiny hexagonal crystal that look like diamonds. You move closer and touch the crystals with your fingers.

"Hey Piver, are these blue diamonds?"

Piver slides over and has a look. "Sure looks like it."

Another layer of rock is a solid band, translucent like glass and two feet thick. The rock is so clear you can see right into it and … That is when you see a pair of eyes looking back at you.

"Piver this rock is looking back at me!"

Piver laughs. "Geebus, that's your reflection silly!"

As you look at the rock, Piver giggles like a madman. Then he calls to the other miners. "Hey, guess what? The rock is looking back!"

You can feel your face redden. But how were you to know? You look again. This time the rock blinks. But you didn't blink. Then you see teeth, large and gleaming. A shimmering crystal claw reaches towards you from inside the rock.

You try to run, but one of the claws snags your uniform. You are trapped.

The rock feels liquid as you are pulled into it. You try to yell out but it's too late. As you are absorbed into the cliff face you suddenly feel peaceful. Like you are part of everything around you.

Don't worry, the stranger's voice inside your head says. *You are one of us now.*

You see Piver from inside the rock and try to shout a warning, but your mouth won't open. Then the magma in the nearest crater rises up and begins to overflow. The miners are running, but the magma is rising too fast. You close your eyes and let the warmth sweep over you.

Unfortunately, this part of your story is over. You've been swallowed by a strange silica based life force very different to your own. However you can always try another path, maybe you'll have better luck.

It is time to make one of three choices. Do you:

Go back to the very beginning of the story and try another path? **P1**

Or

Go back to your last decision and stay at the top of the canyon? **P107**

Or

Go to the list of choices and start reading from another part of the story? **P204**

You have decided to stay at the top of the canyon.

"I think I'd better stay up here," you tell Piver. "I don't want too many people down there at once."

Piver looks disappointed but he's never one to stay low for long. "Well I'd better start lifting some of the crystals out of the canyon then. Looks like it's going to be a fair bit."

You train your scope on the miners working below and see they've dug quite a pile of tyranium already.

"And we don't want to be out here after dewfall," you say.

As Piver goes off to help with the winching, you speak to Gagnon who has been standing guard with some of the other sliders. "Any signs of life?" you ask.

"Nothing so far. Still I get a feeling I'm being watched."

You look around at the foliage crowding the rocky ridge. Are those plants closer than they were before? "Let's not be greedy, eh?" you say to Gagnon. "Once we've got a decent load we'll start zipping back up to where we camped last night. No point pushing our luck."

Gagnon agrees. "I'll get Villum and the others to start cutting steps and get a few zip lines strung up to save us time later."

"Good thinking," you say. "Assuming you can wake Villum up, the lazy sod."

"Oh I'll wake him up easily enough," Gagnon says, pulling out his anchor bolt gun. "Nothing like a big bang to get a Lowlander's attention."

The next couple of hours are spent hoisting crystals out of the canyon and packing the sledges. The miners are in good spirits and quite pleased with their haul.

"We'll leave the platform behind for next time," Piver says. "I'm sure with these results the council will want to send another expedition back here."

Just as your troop is about to move off, there is a low rumble from underground. "Anchors in!" you yell.

The lead slider of each sledge pulls his anchor gun out of his belt and fires a bolt into the rock. With a quick loop a tether is tied around the anchor bolts securing the sledges to the slippery rock.

As the rumbling gets stronger, even the diamond dust on the sledge's runners doesn't prevent the sledges from slipping sideways down the hill to the limit of their tethers. Below, you can hear parts of the canyon wall crumbling away and crashing like glass to the canyon floor.

You know you've got to move fast when you smell fart and look over to see that the pangos are lying on the bottom of Dagma's cage. A pale pink mist is rising up over the lip of the canyon.

"Gas!" you yell.

Thankfully after one last shake the rumbling stops.

"Get moving, everyone, or we'll suffocate!"

Tethers are released and zip lines attached to the cables run up the hill earlier. The powerful zippers pull the sledges at a steady walking pace up the slick black rock of the ridge and before long you leave the stench of gas behind.

"Geebus," Piver says. "Just as well we weren't still in the canyon."

The little engineer is right. If you hadn't been satisfied with a modest load of crystals, some of your team would still have been on the canyon floor beneath the layer of deadly gas. The thought of losing so many of your troop gives you shivers.

You sigh and look back up the mountain. It's a long climb back to Tyron Pass.

With the extra weight on the sledges, climbing is slow. Villum, well aware of how close everyone was to getting caught by the cloud of gas finally seems to have some energy and is running his step cutter at full power. Piver helps him, becoming more and more familiar with the machine's operation.

As winches hum, and zip lines buzz, the sledges are pulled higher and higher up the ridge.

But even with everyone working at full pace, you soon realize you're not going to make it to your previous camp before dewfall.

"Keep an eye out for somewhere to stop," you say to

Gagnon. "Everyone's exhausted and it's getting late."

Ten minutes later Gagnon calls a halt. He tethers his sledge and slides over to the edge of the ridge where the shiny black rock meets a tangle of vines and trees. "I saw a strange reflection in the foliage. I'm going to check it out."

You wait as Gagnon disappears into the bush. When he doesn't reappear after a couple of minutes you signal Dagma and Shoola, to go over and investigate.

Just as they reach the bush line Gagnon reappears. "Come look at this," he calls out. "You're not going to believe your eyes."

As you detach your harness and slide over towards Gagnon, Piver arrives at your side.

"Come with me," Gagnon says turning a walking back between the shrubbery.

Curious, you and the others follow as he leads you out onto a spur looking down the valley to the east. Way off in the distance, nestled at the bottom of the mountain is a small settlement.

"So there are people living this side of the mountains," Piver says.

"Looks like it," you say. "But what caused the reflection you saw, Gagnon?"

Gagnon points to a small bird hovering above you. Its body is covered in fine metallic feathers. The bird's wings flap so fast you can barely see them moving and its eyes rotates in and out like the magnifying lens on your scope.

"Geebus," Piver says. "It's a robot and it's watching us. It must come from whoever is living in that community down there."

You look at the hummingbot and wonder if it can hear you. Maybe you should relay a message to the little bird's owner. Let them know that you come in peace and that they have nothing to fear.

"Come on let's get going," you say. "As much as I'd like to stay, we need to find a place to camp before dewfall."

You leave the sight of the distant settlement behind and carry on up the ridge. Half an hour before dewfall Gagnon spots a flattish area just west of the ridge and you and your sliders make camp.

The next morning, after another three hours climbing, your troop finally reaches Tyron Pass and stands looking over the Black Slopes towards home.

Then you notice the hummingbot is back. This time is has something in its beak. As the little bird nears, you see it's a delicate flower, tiny and perfect. The bird drops the flower in your palm and then flutters back a few yards away to watch your reaction.

You take the tiny flower between your thumb and forefinger and bring it to your nose. Its scent is the most intoxicating thing you've ever smelled. You look up at the bird and smile. "Thank you," you say, not knowing if the bird can hear you or not. "Please tell your owner we will come back soon to talk trade."

The bird tweets twice, does a quick loop the loop and flies off.

You turn to Gagnon. "I think it understood, don't you?"

"Yip," Gagnon says. "Looks like we'll be back this way sooner than we thought."

You pass the flower to Gagnon who takes a whiff. Then he passes it to Piver.

Piver lifts the flower to his nose and without even realizing it, rises up onto his toes as he inhales the heady scent. "Geebus!" he says. "That's the best smell ever!"

Congratulations this part of your story is over. You've had a successful mission, retrieved a load of crystals, and found a friendly new civilization on the far side of the mountains. Well done. But have you followed all the paths this book has to offer? Have you been to Mount Kakona or fought off the morph rats?

It is time to make another decision. Do you:

Go back to the very beginning of the story and try another path? **P1**

Or

Go to the list of choices and start reading from another part of the story? **P204**

You have decided to allow Drexel to climb the Tryon Cliffs.

You have every faith in Piver's skill as an engineer, but it never hurts to have a plan B.

After glancing up at the towering cliffs, you look back at Drexel. "Are you sure about this? Who will lead the climbing team on Mount Kakona if you fall?"

"I'm not planning on falling," Drexel says. "Besides, I'll put in anchors every twenty feet or so."

You rub the back of your neck as you think. "What about someone to help in case you get into trouble? Sliders usually work as a team."

"All I need is someone here at the bottom to send up more line and bolts," Drexel says. "I'll be fine doing the climbing. Once I get to the top, I can haul up a winch and hoist everyone up."

"Okay," you say. "And if the drilling goes as planned we can meet you on the other side."

Drexel smiles. "Deal."

Drexel wastes no time in getting the gear he needs for his attempt to be the first person to scale the Tyron Cliffs.

Meanwhile, Piver has the drill in position and four of the strongest expedition members ready to start the physical task of turning the drill. Each of the four pushers sits in a line with their feet stretched out before them. Their feet rest on footpads linked to the shaft through a series of pulleys. With each push of their feet, belts from the pulleys rotate the shaft. With four people pushing and the gearing of the pulleys, the shaft rotates fast.

Linked to the end of the shaft is the diamond drill bit which claws its way into the rock with every turn. The rubble is hauled back out of the hole by others using a small conveyor belt that sends the debris sliding off into a crevasse further down the slope.

Dagma sits in the lead seat nearest the cliff. She'll be the one the other pushers try to keep up with.

Dagma counts, "One, two, three, four," as she pushes, one foot after the other.

As one pusher tires, another takes their place. Highlanders take great pride in being able to outlast their fellow sliders. And now that Lowlanders are here, the competition will be hard fought and the tunnel will be drilled in record time.

In between counts, Dagma rallies the other pushers and munches on hydro bars to keep her energy levels up. After an hour, the first changeover happens. One of the Lowlanders is exhausted in the thin mountain air. Another quickly slots into his place to keep the drill turning.

"How's it going Piver?" you yell over the grinding of the drill. "Are we going to make it through before the bit gets too dull?"

Piver nods. "Only three more hours I reckon. The bit should last eight."

"That's good news," you say. "Three hours is quicker than I expected."

You step back from the cliff face and look up to where Drexel is making steady progress up the cliff. He's put in half a dozen anchor bolts so far and is about to put in another. Then, once the new bolt is secured, he attaches his harness to it and starts climbing again.

Drexel's climbing technique is impressive. His legs are powerful and he uses them to great effect by kicking his toe studs into the glossy black rock and then pushing his body upwards. In each hand he holds a sturdy pick of high-quality needle crystals. These give him grip wherever he finds a flaw in the rock, however tiny. Then once he's made ten yards or so, he puts in another bolt to protect his position in case of a fall.

Trodie watches Drexel climb. "He's good. You sliders certainly know your stuff up here."

You smile at Trodie's compliment. "It's what we've trained all our lives for."

"I look forward to giving you a tour of the Lowlands sometime," Trodie says. "Have you ever ridden on the water? We have floating gardens you know and boats for catching fish. Fish aren't as tasty as pangos, but when smoked over newly cut crackleberry branches they're not too bad."

"Water and the Highlands are usually a bad mix," you say. "Up here whole troops can be sent to the bottom by a sudden storm."

Trodie nods his understanding. "But in the Lowlands we don't have black glass. The soil is soft and easy to walk on. You must come down and try it some time."

After promising to do just that, you go over and see how Gagnon is getting on.

He looks up as you approach. "I've checked my calculations. The target looks good."

"Excellent," you say. "Drexel's doing well too."

"I need some exercise," Gagnon says, giving you a sideways glance. "Fancy a race on the foot pads?"

You look over towards the drilling machine and notice that a couple of the pushers are tiring. "Okay you're on. Loser has to empty the latrine bucket."

Emptying the latrine bucket is the worst job while on expedition, but it has to be done. You've always respected leaders who were prepared to do the smelly jobs alongside those of lower rank. Respect in the Highlands is earned and not given without good reason.

Gagnon gives you a confidant laugh. "You asked for it!"

The two of you slide over to the drill and tap the two exhausted pushers on the shoulder.

"Time for a rest," you say. "Go have some broth."

Dagma is still pushing after three hours. She's slowing down a little, but even so her pace is hard to keep up with. You and Gagnon fall into step. Left. Right. Left. Right. One, two, three, four.

"Come on push!" Dagma yells down the line. "Outlast me and I'll empty the stink bucket!"

Shoola has just completed a break so she taps another weary slider on the shoulder and rejoins the race. "I'm in too."

Suddenly the race takes on a new urgency. The first one who stops, empties the bucket. One of the other sliders gets out a broth pot and starts keeping rhythm by clanging it with his harness buckle. Others gather around to watch and to cheer for their favorite.

Meanwhile at the cliff face, Piver is pumping a mixture of diamond dust and water onto the drill bit to keep it cool and others struggle to keep up with shifting the rubble out of the hole. With the race on, the drill bit is rotating at twice its normal rate and the tunnel is getting longer and longer by the minute.

After two hours your legs start to cramp. Sweat pours down your back. Dagma and Shoola grit their teeth and push like crazy, each determined to outdo the other. Gagnon's face is flushed and he is breathing heavy. You're sure that any minute now, he'll throw his hands up in defeat and you'll have won.

"Stop!" Piver yells, throwing a lever that disengages

YOU SAY WHICH WAY

the drive shaft. "We're through!"

Suddenly the resistance on the footpads is gone. You lean back and gasp for breath.

Gagnon wipes his forehead and looks over at you. "Lucky we had to stop. I just about had you there."

"Yeah right! Is that why your face looks redder than a pango's beak?"

"Come on everyone," Piver says, ignoring the banter. "Help me pull this drill out."

The drive is disconnected and the drilling machine is dragged back through the perfectly round hole in the cliff.

You slap Piver on the back. "Good work my friend. I suppose we can tell Drexel to come back down now."

"Let's nip through and have a look at what's on the other side first," Piver says. "It might be impassable for all we know."

Piver's making good sense. The terrain on the far side of the tunnel needs to be negotiated by sledges. If that's not possible you'll have to rethink everything.

You wave your arm. "Come on Gagnon, Piver and I are going to see where your tunnel has come out."

You grab your guide stick, put on your headlamp and push your way over to the tunnel entrance. The tunnel walls are almost smooth with only a faint trace of the drill's rotation etched into the surface. A small circle of light, like a moon in the night sky, burns bright at the far end of the blackness.

"Righto, follow me," you say to Piver and Gagnon. "Let's see what we've got."

You step into the tunnel and clip your boots together. Your legs feel like jelly after all the pushing, but as soon as you crouch into the familiar slider's stance and shove off with your stick, you feel the power return to your muscles.

As you slide, the roof of the tunnel is only inches above your head. With its floor being level there is no danger of going too fast and losing control, but about halfway in, when your headlamp picks up a change in the rock's color, you drag your hook and screech to a halt.

"Look here," you say, pointing to a spot on the tunnel's wall. "This rock is more blue than black. It looks similar to tyranium but…"

Piver has the most mining experience. He shines his headlamp onto the lighter section of rock and pulls a small pick from his utility belt. With a short chopping motion, he digs the tip of his pick into the pale rock. "It's hard alright, but not hard enough."

"Worth mining?" you ask.

Piver shakes his head. "The crystals haven't formed enough to be of any use on black glass. Give it another thousand tons of pressure and a million or so years."

You shrug. "That's a shame, it would have saved us a long slide." Then with a big push, you glide the last 15 yards to the end of the tunnel.

The terrain beyond the tunnel is reasonably level, but frequent earthquakes have caused the rock to split, creating long crevasses in the otherwise smooth surface. Still, it looks passable. If the cracks had been running across the slope, then going any further would be impossible. At least these crevasses are running in the same directions as you want to travel and there is flat rock between them.

Off in the distance, rising in a perfect cone, is Mount Kakona. Around the volcano's peak hovers a ring of cloud. A red river of lava runs down its left flank.

"Look, the mountain's creating its own weather," you tell Piver and Gagnon as they come to stand beside you. "The only clouds in sight are around Kakona's summit."

You learned a bit about volcanoes while in Slider School and know that the rain that falls on a volcano's warm upper slopes doesn't take long to evaporate. Then it condenses into clouds again, creating a continuous cycle.

Piver looks up at Kakona's peak. "How are we meant to climb that?"

"Carefully," you say giving the engineer a wink. "Very, very carefully."

Gagnon has his scope out looking for a course through the tricky terrain ahead of you. "At least most of the crevasses are running north south," he says. "As long as we only have to bridge one or two of them, we might get there."

"Why don't you start marking a trail?" you say. "We'll go back and get the others."

Gagnon nods. "Good idea. If we're going to reach the base of Mount Kakona today we're going to have to make good time."

With that Gagnon pulls out his chalk bag and covers the crystal end of his guide stick in bright red powder. Now, whenever Gagnon pushes with his stick, he'll leave a mark for the sledges to follow.

You slap Gagnon on the arm. "Be careful. We'll catch up as quickly as we can."

With that you and Piver push your way back through the tunnel. When you emerge at the other end your troop is waiting anxiously to hear what you've found and Drexel is near the top of the cliff.

You gather everyone together. "The bad news is that there are crevasses between us and the volcano, but the good news is the cracks run north to south so we can slide in between them and will only have to build bridges when two crevasses merge. Gagnon's off scouting a trail so let's get loaded up and move out. We've got a long slide this afternoon."

A hum of excitement buzzes around your troop as gear is strapped down and the sliders connect their harnesses to the sledges. The drill is left behind to reduce weight. With Gagnon out scouting, you decide to take the front harness on the lead sledge yourself. Once everyone is ready you give a big push with your stick and maneuver the sledge into the tunnel.

The diameter of the tunnel is only just big enough to take a sledge. Those riding on top have to duck down so their heads don't scrape the roof. When you emerge on the far side, members of the expedition gasp at the sheer beauty of the volcano in the distance.

As if on cue, Mount Kakona belches out a blast of steam and you feel a slight tremor run through the rock beneath your feet.

"Geebus!" Piver says. "This is going to be interesting."

You smile at the little engineer. "Interesting is putting it mildly."

"Woot! Woot!" Drexel calls from high on the slope behind you. Now he's got a steep slide to get down to your position.

But with skills taught in Slider School, Drexel has no problem. He swoops down the rock in a series of tight S-turns, shifting his weight from one side to the other, his knees bent and guide stick tucked tight under his arm, applying drag as required. The screech of his diamond hook echoes across the landscape and the distinctive swish of his boots cutting turns in the black glass slope is music to your Highland ears.

Drexel skids to a stop beside you. "I see you got

through okay."

You nod. "And you've become the first to scale the Tyron Cliffs. Well done."

Drexel gives you a big grin. "I'll have to give some of the credit to Piver for designing his hand-held launcher. I would have struggled on the last bit without it."

As Drexel goes to thank Piver, you take out your scope and look for Gagnon. The red trail leads between two huge crevasses and then disappears behind a narrow pressure ridge.

"Let's move out," you say, waving your arm. "Keep your hooks at the ready and watch out for the unexpected."

"Woot, woot!" the sliders yell.

You give a big shove with your stick and feel the sledge start to move. Once you gain some momentum, it's easy to keep the heavy sledge moving on the incredibly slippery rock. Every ten yards or so you pass a red mark.

For almost an hour you follow Gagnon's trail, the red marks getting fainter as you go. Then, after coming around a small pinnacle, you see him silhouetted against the sky. He's come to a stop on a narrow triangle of rock where the two crevasses merge into one.

You slide up to his position. "Bridge building time, eh?"

Gagnon nods. "But which side do we take? Left or

right?"

You look up at Kakona. Taking the left side of the crevasse will give you a more direct path to the mountain's base, but it also means you'll end up on the side of the volcano where the lava is flowing. If you take the right-hand side of the crevasse, the route looks longer, but you'll be further away from any potential eruption. Or will you?

It is time to make a decision. Do you:

Go left towards the lava? **P132**

Or

Take the right hand side away from the lava? **P135**

You have decided to trust that Piver can drill through the cliffs.

"Sorry Drexel, I'm going to stick with our original plan."

"But—"

You shake your head. "Look, if you want to help, I suggest you use your leg muscles and help power the drill. Piver's looking for volunteers in case you haven't heard."

Drexel looks downcast, but then brightens up. "If the drill breaks can I have a go?"

You shrug. "Sure."

By the time Drexel gets to the drilling machine, the seats for the pushers that will power the drill are already full and a line has formed of those wanting to take their turn as others become weary. As always, competition to be the one who keeps peddling longest is enthusiastic. Dagma and Shoola are already giving each other a hard time and the drilling hasn't even started yet.

Once Piver has all the pulleys connected, he engages the drill and the pusher start pressing the footpads down — left, then right, then left again, one after the other. As the pushers work the pedals, the shaft rotates and turns the drill bit which grinds into the black glass of the Tyron Cliffs.

Those who aren't pushing, or standing in line, are doing other jobs around the site. A fine slurry of water and diamond dust needs to be directed onto the drill bit to keep it cool, and the debris from the drilling needs to be directed downhill towards a crevasse for disposal.

The drilling goes on for hours. Sliders and Lowlanders alike take a turn on the footpads. Some push for an hour, others exhausted themselves by trying to go too fast and are swapped out quickly. Dagma, her legs pumping in a steady rhythm goes on and on tirelessly. Her years acting as break on Highland sledges have been a good training ground for this activity.

You are about to nod off when you hear a commotion near the drill site. When you look up Piver is waving his arms.

You jump down from the sledge and slide over. "What's going on, Piver?" you ask.

The little engineer looks worried. "We've hit a pocket of something, we need to pull the drill out and see what's going on."

You watch on anxiously as Piver and his team slowly withdraw the long shaft from the hole in the cliff. Then finally, as the bit itself appears, Piver checks that the diamond teeth are okay and then straps on a headlamp.

"I'm going in," Piver says, taking a step into the hole. Then he giggles. "If I'm not back in a week send out a search party."

"Nah," you say joining in the joke. "We'll just plug the hole and move on."

But as Piver slides off into the darkness you realize you're holding your breath. You move closer to the opening and stick your head inside. Off in the distance you can see the reflection of Piver's lamp. Then you hear a faint yelp and the light disappears.

"Piver? Stop fooling around!" you yell.

Nothing.

"Piver! Turn your light back on. That's an order!"

Still nothing.

You turn to the others. "Something's happened to Piver. Sliders ready!"

"Can I help?" asks Trodie.

"Just keep an eye on the sledges," you say. "And pass me another cable. Sliders never leave one of their own on the slopes regardless of the danger."

You, Dagma and Gagnon clip on to a cable and slide forward into the tunnel, your guide sticks pointing forward in a defensive position. Drexel and Shoola feed out cable. The Lowland contingent stand watching, not knowing what to do in this unfamiliar environment.

"What's happened?" Dagma asks. "Crevasse?"

You shrug. "I don't know but we're about to find out."

The tunnel is dark, even with your headlamp on. The black rock doesn't reflect much light and your eyes take a while to adjust. As your pupils dilate and your vision comes into focus, Piver is nowhere to be seen.

"Where's he gone?" you mutter. "This is impossi—"

Then you hear a faint echo. You slide cautiously forward then feel yourself falling. "Brake!" you yell.

There is a screeching of hooks from above and your harness jerks tight. Next thing you know you are swinging in space at the end of the cable.

"I meant to warn you about that," Piver says.

You look down and see Piver crouched on the ground about ten feet below you.

"You okay?"

"Keep your knees bent and relax," Piver says with a smile. "Slider rule number one when falling into an unknown void."

"You just made that up!" you say, relieved your friend is alright. "Where the heck are we?"

"In a massive lava tube by the looks of it," Piver says. "They can run for miles. Our tunnel must have clipped the top of it."

Above your head you hear the sound of anchor bolts going in. Then, a moment later, Dagma zips down a cable and comes to a halt beside you. "I see you found our little friend."

"And more," you say. "Piver's fallen into a lava tube. The perfect place to find tyranium crystals."

"Hey, lower me down a bit more," you yell to the sliders above. "I want to check this place out."

When you've got both feet back onto solid ground you

unclip your harness and shine your light down the tube in each direction. "This thing is huge!" you say.

Dagma hands you the chemical light she's brought down with her. "Here take this. It's a million moth power. Should brighten things up a bit."

You take the chemical-light and flip the switch. A beam of light six inches wide stabs into the darkness, spreading out as it goes. Twenty yards away, the walls are flecked with pinpoints of reflected light.

"Those sparkles look like gold or copper," Piver says. "If that's the case, tyranium won't be far away."

The three of you move cautiously down the tube, scanning the walls as you go. Then you see them, needle crystals, hanging from the ceiling about twenty yards away, a vast row them stretching as far as you can see.

"Tyranium!" Piver says. "Squillions of it!"

"Grazillions," Dagma says, with a chuckle.

"Pazillions," you say, making up your own word for the massive cluster of crystals and joining in the fun. "That, my friends, is an impressive amount of rock."

Piver slides forward for a closer look. "Geebus, you're not wrong there. Looks like it's good quality too."

You turn off the chemical light and point your headlamp up at the ceiling. With all the crystals reflecting, it's like looking at the night sky only brighter. Everyone is speechless.

After a minute you break the silence. "We'd better get

back and tell the others what we've found," you say.

Once you're clipped on to the cable again, the sliders up top pull you back to the surface.

The expedition members are buzzing with excitement after hearing what you've discovered. Only once or twice in a generation is such a rich deposit found. This one will break records, of that you have no doubt. Although the majority of the minerals will go to the council, there is always a small proportion that goes to the expedition members that make the discovery. A small piece of a very, very large pie, is still a lot of pie.

The next few days are spent rigging pulleys and bringing the mined crystals to the surface. Once the sledges are loaded to capacity, your group starts back.

Trekking back with heavy sledges takes time and effort, but slow and safe is better than losing a sledge so close to success.

Three days later, from near the top of Long Gully, you see a familiar sight. "Look, the Pillars of Haramon!"

The glimmering pinnacles shimmer in early afternoon sun, reflecting beams of light around the valley. In the distance the Lowlands, with their patchwork fields of crops stretches off to the turquoise sea on the horizon. A line of towering black peaks runs off to the east like the spine of some ancient monster.

Trodie comes to a screeching halt beside you and looks down at his homeland beyond the pillars. "Hard to believe anything could be so beautiful, isn't it?"

"Does it make you feel small?" you ask.

"Smaller than small," he says with a smile. "And luckier than you'll ever know."

Congratulations, this part of your story is over. You've led a successful expedition, discovered a new source of tyranium crystals, and made new friends. However, have you followed all the paths the story takes?

It is time to make a decision. Do you:

Go back to the very beginning of the story? **P1**

Or

Go to the list of choices and start reading from somewhere else? **P204**

You have decided to take the left hand side of the crevasse.

"Let's go left," you say.

"What about the lava?" Gagnon asks. "Aren't you worried about that river of molten rock?"

You laugh. "I'm not planning on swimming in it. Besides, the whole reason we're here is tyranium crystals and if they're going to be found without having to dig for them, we'll need to look around the active vents or find an old lava tube."

Gagnon smiles. "Just be careful. Get too hot and Dagma might think you're a roasted pango and take a bite out of your leg."

"I heard that!" Dagma says with a big toothy grin. "Watch it or you'll be the one I roast over the lava flow."

Gagnon snorts. "For someone who can get lost in their sleeping hammock, you'd be lucky to find a lava flow before it snuck up on you and melted your boots. There's more than one reason they put you on the back of the sledge you know."

Shoola and a couple of the other sliders laugh along with Gagnon. Dagma takes the ribbing well though, she's been right through Slider School with Gagnon and their banter is always good humored.

After the laughter subsides and with the decision made about which direction to go, Piver and the other sliders get to work unloading the pipes, brackets and bolts needed to construct the makeshift bridge.

The other sliders are quick to follow Piver's instructions, so it isn't long before the ladder-bridge is maneuvered across the crevasse and anchored in position. Then the sledges are pushed across.

"Geebus! That's a long way down," Piver says from halfway across. "Don't look down unless you want to fill your pants."

Once everyone is safely on the other side, the bridge is broken down and reloaded onto the sledges.

"Good work everyone," you say. "Let's get moving. We've got a lot of rock to cover before we can make camp."

Gagnon takes off in the lead again, but it isn't long before you wonder if you've made a major mistake. The strip of rock you're sliding on is getting narrower and narrower the further you go and the crevasses on each side are getting wider and deeper. At some points, there is barely enough rock for the sledge's runners to grip on to.

When the terrain begins to slope downhill, sliding on the narrow strip of rock gets really tricky. The screech of hooks from Dagma and Shoola, acting as brakes, is constant as they try to keep the speed under control. Rumblings under foot as the mountain spews more lava adds to the tension.

The next time two crevasses merge you build your bridge so you can head further west, away from the lava, and more importantly, away from the continual earthquakes shaking the ground under your feet. The last thing you want is for one of your sledges to be jolted off course and tumble into a crevasse.

Nerves are on edge as you spend the afternoon sliding, building bridges and watching the volcano erupt. As you get closer the mountain looms larger and steeper and becomes way more dangerous looking. Every few minutes a new burst of smoke and steam shoots skyward, peppering the area with grit and tiny pebbles.

About an hour before dewfall you finally break free of the crevasse field and slide out onto a smooth plateau of rock. The plateau is reasonably flat. Along one side is an old lava flow rising sixty or seventy feet above the surrounding terrain. Some of the cave openings in the old flow look interesting. Rocks as small as your fist and as large as a sledge litter the plateau around you.

Your troop is tired and needs rest before they try to scale Mount Kakona tomorrow in search of tyranium crystals. It is time to make a decision. Do you:

Make camp on the plateau? **P145**

Or

Go check out the caves? **P149**

You have decided to take the right hand side away from the lava.

You point to the northeast. "Once we're across the crevasse, let's go away from the lava. It'll be safer."

Piver looks at you and chuckles.

"What are you laughing about?" you ask him.

"You said 'safer'. That's like saying jumping off a 100 foot cliff is safer than jumping off a 200 foot cliff. If this baby blows, we're in the bucket whichever way we go."

"I disagree," Gagnon pipes in. "The eastern side's upwind of the volcano. Less chance of getting gassed if that monster belches out hydrogen sulfide."

"Yeah, Piver," you say. "I'm saving you from death by volcano fart so stop complaining."

"Me complain? Never! Besides, I've got no sense of smell. If the worst happens I'll just lay down and go to sleep forever while all of you are on your knees gagging and ralphing your guts out."

A cold shiver runs up your spine. "Thanks for that thought. Remind me to leave you at home next time."

Piver cocks a leg and lets off an explosive fart. "What? And miss out on my sweet music?"

"Holy moly, Piver!" you say pinching your nose. "That smells worse than the south end of a northbound pango. You're on the last sledge from now on, stinky pants."

Piver giggles and slides off to organize the equipment

he and the other engineers will need to build a bridge across the crevasse.

About an hour later, once the sledges and members of the expedition are over the chasm, your group slides off towards the volcano. Maybe you'll get lucky and discover an old lava tube full of tyranium crystals on this less active side of the volcano. If not, you'll have to risk investigating further west. Then it will be a matter of avoiding the lava as well as rocks and gas volcanoes tend to eject at random.

Another hour and your group finally clears the crevasse field. Here, nearer the base of the mountain, the cracks in the ground have been filled in with lava from recent eruptions and is almost back to it normal smoothness. Only the odd slump in the surface remains to show where the massive crevasses once were.

One of these slumps still has some water in it from the last rain. It's only two feet deep, but it gives everyone a chance to fill their containers and drink their fill.

The only other irregularities in the smooth landscape is the occasional pressure ridge, where massive plates of rock have been forced together, tilting one plates upwards as the other plate dives beneath it. These ridges give you an awesome respect for the power of nature. They also expose a different strata of rock and are of immense interest to the miners.

Most of these ridges you can work your way around,

but as the ground starts to rise in its sweep towards the mountain's summit, a particularly large pressure ridge blocks your path. This plate of hardened lava, nearly 30 feet thick, has been push up and over until it's overhanging.

Gagnon pulls out his scope and starts looking for a way around the obstruction but the ridge runs for quite some distance in each direction. "Might have to winch ourselves over."

You call Drexel over. "How are you at climbing overhangs?"

Drexel borrows Gagnon's scope and scans the huge slab. "Better yet, I'll just launch a cable over the top and zip up. I should be able to negotiate the overhang, then winch the rest of you up and over."

"What about the sledges?" you ask.

Drexel shakes his head. "No way are we going to get the sledges over this, they'll just jam at the top."

Drexel's suggestion is the sensible option. The ground is getting steeper with every step and drilling through the ridge is out of the question.

"Piver!" you call out. "Get a launcher set up and shoot a cable over the top. The rest of you, get packing. Take only what you can carry. Enough for two days."

With excitement, everyone starts sorting gear and equipment. By the time Dagma has finished, her pack is bulging with energy bars.

With a swoosh of compressed air, Piver sends a grapple flying over the pressure ridge. Then he reels it in tight, making sure it's well snagged on the other side. Drexel is quick to attach his harness and pull the trigger on his zipper. Everyone watches as he rises up the line. Once at the top, he swings a leg onto the lip and pulls himself up and over the overhang.

"Okay let's get the lightweight winch hooked up," Piver says.

Once Drexel has hauled the winch up and attached it safely to the rock above, the expedition members are lifted, one by one, up and over the obstruction.

After overseeing the operation from below, you are last to clip on to the cable. The ride up gives you a great view of the surrounding area. When you reach the top, strong hands help you over the lip.

On solid rock again, you pull out your scope and search the slopes of Kakona for any signs of old lava tubes. They are hard to pick out on the smooth black surface as shadows tend to look just like the rock.

But when you see a faint glow coming from a spot about half a mile up the mountain, you wonder if what you're seeing is the light from a moon moth colony or something else. Moths always nest underground, in the mouths of caves, tunnels, or hopefully in this case, the entrance to a tyranium filled lava tube.

"Okay, I see something," you say. "Rope up everyone

and keep your hooks ready."

Climbing even a gentle slope would be impossible without the diamond studs on the heels of your boots and your guide stick. But steep ground is made slowly, and anchor bolts need to be put in every twenty yards or so for protection. A few of the Lowlanders, unused to traveling on black glass, have minor slips, but your Highland sliders are quick to arrest their fall.

After a hard climb you finally reach the source of the light. It isn't moon moths, but something much stranger. What you first thought might be light coming from a moth colony, is actually sunlight reflecting off a robot, the likes of which you've never seen.

"What the heck is that?" you say, looking at the snake-like contraption.

Piver slide over for a look. "I think it's a self propelled drill. See, this hole is far too smooth to be a lava tube."

"Okay, but who built it? Trodie, is this something you Lowlanders have built?"

Trodie shakes his head. You can tell by the confusion on Trodie's face that he's telling the truth.

"Looks like it's broken down," Piver says. "The teeth on the front are all twisted out of shape and it's starting to deteriorate in the weather."

Gagnon slides over and looks into the tunnel the machine has drilled. "Maybe we should go in and have a look? There could be crystals down there."

You shrug. "But who would abandon something of such value? Did they find crystals, is that why this machine is still here?" You climb up a few steps to get a better look at the abandoned machine.

Then, as you are about to send a couple sliders down the tunnel to check it out, a waft of something rank hits you. At first you think Piver has farted again, but then you hear a familiar slurping sound, like suction cups being pushed on and off a slightly damp surface and the clacking of sharp teeth.

"Morph rats!" Shoola yells. "Directly uphill!"

Up the slope, about a hundred yards away, you see a wave of the hairless horrors, their teeth gnawing at the air, the slime on their wrinkled bodies reeking of fart.

"Sliders, to me! Emergency wedge formation!" you yell. "Lowlander get in behind."

The six sliders on the mission quickly climb to your position and form themselves into a wedge, each with the hook end of their guide stick pointing forwards towards the threat. Dagma, being the strongest, positions herself at the pointy end of the wedge.

As the plague of rats rolls down the slope toward your position, your troop braces itself and gets ready to sweep the rats left and right as they move like an unstoppable wave down the mountain.

"What are they doing up so high?" Gagnon says. "This can't be happening."

But happening it is. The wave of slimy rats is moving down the hill, their teeth clacking, the stench growing. And they're coming right at you.

"There are too many!" Dagma yell. "We'll never sweep this many aside!"

Your brain throbs as you work on a solution. There must be something you can do! Then you remember the hole drilled in the slope by the strange machine. Anything is better than getting eaten by morph rats.

"Quick, to the hole," you say.

Everyone breaks formation and slides back to the hole. It is dark inside and you don't know where it leads, but the rats are nearly upon you. You either go down the hole now, or get eaten alive.

"Woot woot!" you yell as you slide into the hole. "Follow me!"

After a quick look at the approaching rats, the others don't hesitate.

Once in the hole, the ground slants steeply and keeping your feet isn't an option. In seconds you find yourself on your backside sliding faster and faster into the darkness. You hear a few woot woots behind you, but your main focus is staring at the blackness and hoping you don't run into anything unexpected. Then you remember your headlamp and reach for the switch.

"Geebus!" you hear Piver yell behind you. "This is freaky!"

The little engineer isn't wrong. This is the scariest thing you've ever done. You think of your family and wonder if you'll ever see them again. As you slide deeper into the mountainside, you feel the heat increase. Will this hole end up in a pool of lava somewhere? Was it the heat that twisted the teeth on the strange drilling machine?

When the tunnel makes a sharp turn to the right you nearly lose your lunch. Someone screams behind you. Or was that your hook dragging? Then the slope steepens again and you're in freefall. You headlamp barely shows you ten yards ahead. Seeing almost makes the experience scarier. You close your eyes for a moment. After what seems like ages, the tunnel's angle lessens, and then, finally, you pop out into the light.

You've come to rest on a flat section of rock that overlooks a lake. Around the lake are domed structures made from triangular pieces of black glass, beyond these are orchards and fields.

"Where are we?" Piver asks as he comes to rest beside you. "And what are those strange constructions?"

"That is a very good question," you say, admiring the beautiful buildings.

There are gasps from the others as they slide to a stop. Gagnon is one of the first to his feet. "Look, someone's coming!"

He's right. A girl about your age is walking towards

your group. She is wide eyed and staring at your group. But her expression is one of curiosity not fear.

"Hello," the girl says. "You must be the ones from the other side of the cliffs."

You step forwards. "So you know about us?"

The girl laughs. "Of course we do. Our robots have had you under observation for ages."

A tiny robotic bird flies near the girl's shoulder. Its lens of an eye zooming in and out as it observes your group.

"Wow!" Piver says. "You make robotic birds too?"

The girl nods. "We make lots of interesting things."

You look up at the high mountains behind you. "So what now?" you ask. "How do we get home?"

"First you need to come and rest. The settlement is preparing a feast to celebrate your arrival."

"A feast?" Dagma says.

"Yes. For our cousins from over the mountains. We're all related you know."

You hesitate. "But…"

"Hey, she said a feast," Dagma is quick to interject. "Let's not disappoint our new friends."

For once, Dagma is right.

The girl smiles. "Once you've eaten and rested, and told us your stories, we'll get you back to your sledges with the tyranium you seek."

"You know about that too?" you ask. "But how?"

The little bird flies to your shoulder, its eye scans you closely, then it flies back to the girl.

"Our tiny friends miss very little," the girl says.

And then as the sun drops below the ridge and you start to feel a dampness in the air, you hear a long blast from a whistle.

"Come, dinner's ready," the girl says. "I hope you brought an appetite with you."

You look over at a grinning Dagma. "Oh yeah. We never travel without one of those."

Congratulations, this part of your story is over. You've discovered a new settlement, been promised the tyranium you seek and are about to enjoy a feast in your honor. Well done.

But have you tried all the paths this story can take?

It is time to make a decision. Do you:

Go back to the beginning of the story and try a new path? **P1**

Or

Go to the list of choices and start reading from another part of the story? **P204**

You have decided to make camp on the plateau.

"Okay let's fire up the burners and get some broth heating," you say. "Piver, would you please get the hammocks and tarps up."

Everyone works together and before long you're sitting around a warm burner with a hot cup of broth in your hands. After getting some food in their bellies your troop is starting to tell stories and joke with each other. Some even sing songs.

As the sun goes down, a light dew falls across the slopes, making it dangerous to move out of camp. Damp rock is way too slippery, even for sliders with guide sticks and diamond-studded boots.

Still, with the anti-slip mats down, and your hammocks and tarps up there is no need to go anywhere. But then just as you're starting to relax, you feel the ground shake and the crash of rocks landing on the slopes around you.

"Eruption!" Gagnon yells as everyone leaps to their feet.

The next big shake knocks you back to the ground and rocks smack into the ground only yards away.

"We're sitting pangos here," Piver says. "We've got to get to the caves or we're going to get flattened."

But how are you going to get to the caves? Dew has fallen and the rock is too slick.

Then, a huge rock smashes one of the sledges into a

million fragments. Your protective tarps and a row of hammocks are taken with it, turning your camp into a disaster zone.

More rocks fall, hitting members of your troop.

As you crawl to your knees, wondering what to do, it is Piver that makes a move.

"Quick, clip on to this," he says picking up a length of cable. Piver fires a couple anchor bolts into the rock and quickly attaches the end of the cable to it.

As another shake shudders through the slope and more rocks crash into your camp, only six of you manage to clip on to Piver's lifeline.

Piver runs the cable through a ring on his harness and then grabs your arm, pulling you to the far right hand side of the camp's safety mats. "Everyone over here, we need to run and throw ourselves off the left side of the mat far as we can. Ready?"

"I hope you know what you're doing," you say.

"Got another plan?" Piver yells. He gives you a stern look. "No I didn't think so. Right on three, two, one go!"

And with that the six of you run as fast as you can and throw yourself onto the slippery rock. At first, as you slide in a straight line, Piver pays out cable. But then, as gravity takes hold and it starts dragging you down, you and the others become the pendulum on the end of a long piece of cable. Suddenly you reach the end of the cable you change direction and start swinging back below the camp and over towards the entrances to the caves in the old lava flow.

You and the others are really moving now, sliding across the rock in a perfect arc. Piver grabs a handheld launcher from his utility belt and points it at the lava flow as your reach the end of your swing. Just as you're group starts to slow, he pulls the trigger and the bolt streaks out and lodges in the rock of the old lava.

"Got it!" Piver says.

After unclipping from the long cable the six of you pull yourselves over to the cave's entrance and duck inside. And not a moment too soon

Another eruption and rocks are landing all over your abandoned camp.

You and the other survivors work your way deeper into the cave, helped by the faint glow of a moon moth colony nesting near the entrance. Once you're well out of the firing line, you sit and shake your head at your mistakes.

You should have realized those rocks on the plateau had been thrown from the volcano. Why didn't you make camp in the safety of the cave from the very beginning? Then you wouldn't have lost half of the members of your expedition and 95 percent of your supplies.

Unfortunately this part of your story is over. You will be doing well just to get back to the Pillars of Haramon, let alone bring any tyranium crystals with you. However you still have a decision to make. There are three choices. Do you:

Go back to your last decision, change your mind and check out the caves? **P149**

Go to the very beginning of the story and try another path? **P1**

Or

Go to the list of choices and try reading from another part of the story? **P204**

You have decided to check out the caves.

"Let's head towards the caves," you tell your group. "There are too many rocks being ejected from Kakona for us to camp out in the open."

As if to illustrate your point, a rock about the size of a fully grown pango slams into the slope not more than 100 yards away.

"Geebus!" Piver says. "Let's get a move on. That was a bit close."

Without wasting any more time, you slide towards the old lava flow. The first couple of caves you find are quite small and don't go into the rock very far. But then you find one that looks more suitable. It has a flat section near its opening for setting up the burners, plenty of room for the sledges, and good spots to hang hammocks. A little way in, the cave meets up with a much larger tunnel that runs up and down the mountain.

"I wonder how far this lava tube goes?" says Gagnon. "It's huge. Who knows, there might even be crystals in it."

You agree with your navigator. "Let's have a bite to eat and a good sleep. We can get some extra lights and go exploring in the morning."

Most of the troop is only interested in food. Unpacking the burners and getting some broth on the heat is always high on the Slider Corps priority list.

You notice that Trodie is particularly interested in the cave. "So, you think this is an old lava tube eh?"

"It's a lava tube alright. See those ridges along the walls? They mark the level of different flows that have come through here."

Trodie runs his hand along one of the distinctive lines in the rock. "So how do you know if it's still active or not?"

You shrug. "That's the problem. You don't. That's why we'll camp in the smaller offshoot near the entrance and not in the main tunnel."

Trodie shakes his head. "I don't know how you Highlanders survive up here. It's so much safer in the Lowlands."

You laugh. "You've got a point. But then life is what you're used to. I can't imagine what living on the flat would be like. It would seem strange without the views, the howling wind and the slick black rock."

Trodie is quiet as he looks off into the darkness. You suspect he's thinking about his home far below. You doubt he's the only one.

Piver breaks Trodie's trance by handing him a steaming cup of broth. "Here you go LoLa, wrap your lips around this."

"Thanks, HiLa," Trodie says in reply, giving the little engineer a wink.

You chuckle under your breath at how well Trodie's

handled Piver's slight insult and wonder if he's made up HiLa on the spot, or if it's a term in common usage down in the Lowlands.

Language, and slang in particular, is an interesting topic, but a sharp twinge in your stomach reminds you how hungry you are. It's been a long hard slide and your nerves have taken a beating today. What you really want is a nice steaming bowl of hydro and a good night's sleep.

Thankfully, the night passes uneventfully, despite being woken by a major rock shower just after climbing into your hammock. It's just as well you chose to camp in the cave, otherwise your group would have been in serious trouble.

The next morning you wake up early. The air outside is fresh and clear. The volcano has taken a nap and has stopped throwing rocks all over the slopes around you. While the rest of the troop sleeps, you decide to strap on a headlamp and check out the main lava tube.

After a quick slide down, and zipping back up, you see that there hasn't been enough pressure for crystals to form. By the time you get back up to the others, Dagma has got the burner going and the troop is sitting around it stuffing their faces.

Grabbing some food, you sit with the others. "Okay everyone, the volcano's taking a break, so let's eat fast and get moving. Who know how long it will be before Kakona blows its top again."

Gagnon looks up. "Don't you want to check out the lava tube?"

"I've just had a look. This tube is too fresh for crystals."

Gagnon looks disappointed, but being the slider he is, he takes the news with his normal calm. "Time to climb a volcano then."

"We'll leave the sledges and free climb from this point," you say. "Pack just enough for two days, nothing more. The terrain is going to get steep and we'll need to move fast."

Within twenty minutes everyone is packed and ready to go. But as you stand in the caves entrance, a massive boom blasts the top fifty feet of Kakona into a million pieces, sending a great plume of steam and rock into the air.

The shock wave from the explosion, hits you a few seconds later, knocking everyone but Dagma and Shoola off their feet.

"Holy moly!" Piver says, dusting himself off.

Then the rain of rocks begins.

"Get back!" you yell.

Rocks and boulders start landing all over the slope. Some are so large they shake the ground when they slam into the slope. Hundreds of thousands of cubic yards of material fall in a wide arc around the mountain creating havoc. Boulders roll like wrecking balls down the slope, crushing everything in their path. Everyone moves deeper into the cave.

As the rocks continued to fall, your group cowers in the main lava tube, hands over heads and thankful for the solid protection over your heads. A few rocks bounce into the cave, but are stopped by the sledges which suffer minor damage.

Finally, when the rocks stopped falling, you and the others move toward the cave's entrance, not quite knowing what you'll find.

When you reach the cave's mouth and look outside, dust fills the air, blocking out the sun's rays. But after a few minutes, the breeze clears the dust away.

Many rocks cover the plateau outside. Only they aren't just rocks. Amongst the basalt and black glass are chunks of tyranium the size of your head. Hundreds of them.

Piver's grin is so wide, he's in danger of splitting his head in two. He runs out and picks up a huge crystal. "It's raining gems, holy moly, it's raining gems," he says as he does a funny little jiggle.

"You're crazy, Piver," you say to the little engineer.

As you exit the cave and walk amongst the material the volcano spat out, you see more tyranium lying on the ground than your troop could carry back with a dozen sledges. It's only the rocks that have landed on flat ground that haven't slid off into the crevasse field further down the mountain. But that's still quite a lot.

But it's when you look up at the mountain, that you realize the magnitude of what just happened. Kakona's once majestic cone is now a row of broken teeth.

It is a time of awe and gratitude. Imagine what would have happened if your troop had been out on the plateau. Not one would have survived. And by the look on everyone's faces, they are well aware of this.

After making some quick repairs, the sledges are loaded with as many crystals as they'll carry, aftershocks rumble under your feet. Everyone works hard in their desire to leave this place as quickly as possible.

"We can't take it all. Leave some for next time people," You say as you inspect the strapping on the sledges yourself. "The last thing we want is an unstable load causing an accident on the way home."

Sliding downhill is always more dangerous. Once a heavy sledge gets moving, it's a hard thing to stop.

Within an hour you've ordered everyone to get ready to move out. They don't need to be told twice. The ground is trembling and lava still flows down the flanks of Kakona.

"That's it, we're ready," Piver says. "Let's go home."

The trip back is slow. Maneuvering the heavy sledges over the bridges takes twice the time. When the Tyron Cliffs appear in the distance everyone's spirits are raised.

"Woot, woot!" the Highlanders call out. "Woot, woot!"

When your group reaches the cliffs, you call a halt. "We'll stay here tonight."

"As least its mainly downhill from here," Trodie says. "I can't say how pleased I'll be to get back to the Pillars."

"And then home eh?" you say. "Back to your family."

Trodie nods. "Yeah, and some flat ground for a change. Up here I feel I'm always on a lean."

After slinging your hammock, you're pleased to take the weight off your sore feet. The slide back to the Pillars of Haramon should be routine, assuming the weather holds.

As you lie back, you wonder if you'll get a star for your efforts. You have no doubt your expedition has exceeded the council's wildest dreams. You also feel you've forged a strong bond with Trodie and the other Lowlanders. This is a real bonus, especially with the Lowlanders and Highlanders struggling to maintain a truce.

The next morning, as you move out, all you can think about is getting everyone home safe. But it isn't until your group reaches the top of Long Gully, for the long slide down to the Pillars of Haramon, that you finally start to relax.

"The Pillars!" Gagnon yells out. "I can see them!"

And then, you can see them too. Never before have the two shimmering black monoliths looked so beautiful. As you sweep down the gulley in a series of S-turns the whole of Petron opens out before you. Past the Pillars, off in the distance, the Lowlands stretch out towards the sea. Petron's smallest moon has risen and sits just above the horizon. The sun in low. Dewfall will be soon. If you hurry, you'll have just enough time to get home.

But despite your rush, for a moment, the expedition slows down and comes to a stop. For almost a minute, the only sound is the faint screeching of a distant pango colony. Then you hear movement beside you. It's Piver.

"Geebus," the engineer says. "Isn't that just the most beautiful site you've ever seen?"

Congratulations, this part of your story is over. You've made it back from the Volcano of Fire and brought a big load of tyranium needle crystals back with you. You've also helped cement friendly relations with the Lowlanders. Well done!

But it is time to make another decision. Do you:

Go back to the beginning and try another path? **P1**

Or

Go to the list of choices and start reading from another part of the book? **P204**

You have decided to go up and around the Tyron Cliffs.

"Well if we've got to climb, we may as well do it while we're fresh," you say.

Gagnon nods. "Righto, it's uphill then. I'll start planning. At least the maps we've got of this side of the mountain aren't too bad."

You nod. "But who knows what we'll find on the other side eh?"

Gagnon smiles. "Well, as the old saying goes, you've got to break open a pango's egg to find out if it's rotten."

Suddenly you hear Piver break out in laughter.

You stab him a look. "What now?"

"That saying is sillier than brain dead pango," Piver says. "Any engineer knows rotten eggs float."

"It's a metaphor, Piver," Gagnon says. "No need to take things so literally."

After the loading has finished, everyone starts the long climb.

Dagma and Shoola lead the charge by climbing a hundred yards, using toe studs and then putting in an anchor bolt. Then the sledges are winched by hand up the slope. Then another slider takes their turn climbing and the others repeat the process.

By mid afternoon you realize you've made a mistake. This is taking far too long. The terrain is too steep for sledges, and even if you did find a load of tyranium, you'd never get a sledge load of the crystal back down the mountain without someone getting injured or worse.

You drop your hook and come to a stop. "Stop everyone, this is crazy. We're going to have to come up with another solution."

Drexel see his opportunity. "Let me try to climb over. It will save us so much time."

You look at Drexel and then up at the sheer wall of black glass. "But it's straight up!"

"It's steep alright, but I reckon it's possible."

"I'm willing to give it a go," Trodie says. "Us Lowlanders can climb too you know."

"Race!" Dagma yells. "Woot! Woot!"

The others on the expedition like the idea too. Everyone likes a race, especially when it means that they can stop climbing for a while and rest their weary legs.

"High, high, high, high!" the Highlanders chant.

"Low, low, low, low!" The Lowlanders reply.

You look at the smiling faces around you. "Okay, looks like we have two contestants who want to be the first to climb the Tyron Cliffs."

Then you think about safety. A race on such a treacherous cliff might tempt one of the climbers into taking one chance too many. You're determined to get home without losing anyone. But what can you do?

You climb onto a sledge and point up. "This is a

dangerous climb and racing is risky. Just getting up this monster cliff will be an amazing effort. But we risk our lives every day on the Black Slopes and it's important that someone manages to climb it. So I'll open the challenge up to anyone who wants to try it."

Trodie and Drexel start sorting out the gear they'll need for the climb. Then you see that Piver is also sorting gear out.

"What the heck do you think you're doing, Piver?" you ask.

Piver looks up from his task. "You did say anyone could climb didn't you?"

"Sure but…"

Then Piver pulls out a couple of his hand launchers, and tucks them into his utility belt. Another couple he stuffs into his jacket. "I have a plan," he says, a big grin on his face. "I may not be the best climber, but I can zip faster than anyone because I'm light."

"You're crazy, Piver," you say. "But I like the way you think."

"High, high, high, high!" the Highlanders chant.

"Low, low, low, low!" the Lowlanders reply.

As the three climbers approach the wall, everyone else gathers around.

Trodie and Drexel are kitted out with the more traditional climbing gear of needle crystal picks, anchor bolts, and lightweight cables. In addition, they each have an extra spike strapped onto the front of their boots.

Piver, despite having nowhere near as much gear as the others, looks relaxed with only a few anchors and some light-weight cable in his pack.

"We'll start the climb when I say go," you say. "I know this is a race, but please be careful. You don't win if you're a messy splat on the rock."

The excitement builds. Everyone is jostling for the best positions to watch the action.

You lift your arm. "On my mark! Three … two … one … Go!"

And with that, Trodie and Drexel start kicking their toe spikes into the rock and swinging their picks. For every two kicks and two chops, the climbers gain a little bit of altitude.

"I said go, Piver!"

"Yeah, I know." Piver turns and walks away from the wall, until he's about 10 yards back. Then he pulls one of his hand launcher out of his jacket and takes aim.

With a hiss of air, a tiny bolt rockets out of the launcher and embeds itself into the rock fifteen meters up. Then to the shock of the other two climbers, Piver pulls the trigger, runs towards the wall, and the hand-launcher zips him up and past them.

"Woot! Woot!" the Highlanders yell."

"Hey!" Drexel says. "That's cheating!"

Piver looks down and giggles. "Show me that in the

rule book, Pango brain!"

While Drexel argues the point, Trodie keeps climbing and moves into second place.

Then Piver's real plan is revealed. He starts pushing himself away from the wall, swinging on the cable. As he come back to the cliff face each time, his short muscular legs act like a coiled spring. The fourth time he springs back, he fires another bolt up the cliff. Then, after removing the first bolt, he zips up. As he repeats the process, he gains altitude and quickly and leaves the other climbers behind.

It doesn't take long before Drexel and Trodie realize that Piver is going to win the climbing race by a huge margin. Not because he's the best climber, but because he had the best plan.

"High, high, high, high!" the Highlanders cheer as Piver nears the top.

Trodie and Drexel decide to save their strength and rappel back down. They leave Piver to continue on to the win.

"Geebus!" Piver cheers as he reaches the top. "I win! Bow before me, lowly Petronians."

"Well done Piver, but cut the boasting. Nobody likes a braggart," you yell up to him. "Now send a line down so the rest of us can get over these cliffs!"

Piver giggles and sends a thin line down to where you are waiting. You tie a stronger cable on to this and he pulls it up and feeds it through a pulley he's anchored to the rock.

"We'll just take one sledge with us from here," you say to your troop. "It will take too much time and energy to haul both of them up."

Just over an hour later your troop is on top of the Tyron Cliffs. On this side of the obstacle, the ground slopes gently down to a reasonably flat plateau. Beyond the plateau, the volcano sweeps up to a mighty cone shrouded in purple mist, and oozing lava.

With only one sledge, you've got plenty of muscle for pulling once your troop has negotiated the slope down to the plateau. A quick change of rig and you've four pullers harnessed up for the ten mile slide to the foot of Kakona.

The only thing that gives you concern are the rocks you see scattered about the otherwise featureless landscape.

"These rocks must have been thrown out of Kakona at some stage," you say to Gagnon, pointing to a shiny black beast the size of the sledge not more than a few hundred yards away. "I'm feeling a little exposed out here. What about you?"

"I was thinking that too," Gagnon says. "Let's just hope Kakona doesn't need to sneeze today."

Half way across the plateau Piver yells for you all to stop. "That boulder over there looks interesting. I want to check it out."

You call for a break while Piver slides over to the rock that's caught his eye.

"I've never see red crystals like this before," he says, inspecting a streak down one side of the boulder. He takes his small blue diamond pick out of his utility belt. "I'll just test how hard it is."

Piver raises the pick and swings it onto the red rock. "Geebus!" Piver says as the pick bounces off the rock and flies out his hand. "It's harder than blue diamond!"

"But that's impossible," you hear one of the others mumble. "Blue diamonds are the hardest thing on the planet."

"Not anymore," Piver says looking for a dent or some other indication of where he hit the rock with his pick. "Not a scratch!"

You walk to the sledge and grab a larger pick. "Here you go Dagma, take a swing and see what you can do."

Dagma is always happy to show off her strength. She unhooks her harness and slides over to the rock with the big pick in her hands. She braces herself, feet wide, heel studs jammed into the black rock at her feet. Then with a roundhouse swing, she takes aim at the red section of rock.

Twang! Clatter, clatter goes the pick as it bounces off the rock and skitters away from where Dagma is standing.

Again Piver checks for a mark. "Nothing!"

"Wow," Trodie says.

"Wow," Shoola says.

"Holy moly," you say. "So what now, Piver? This boulder is too big to fit on the sledge."

"No worries," Piver says. "We'll chop all the basalt off and just load the crystal. Nobody at home is going to believe what we've found."

"So what will we use it for?" you ask.

Piver giggles. "Are you kidding me? We'll be able to drill into black glass twice as fast. We can make tunnels we never dreamed of, make tools to cut steps and form tracks … Geebus, all sorts of stuff."

"But it's not tyranium," you say. "That's what we've been sent to find."

This time Piver's booming laugh echoes across the plateau.

"It's better," he says. "Believe me, the council are going to think this is the best expedition of all time. Look at the size of it."

Gagnon slides over. "Piver's right you know. It wouldn't surprise me if they give you a promotion for this."

Everyone is in good spirits as they work, chipping the basalt off the boulder. In the end, you are left with a red diamond that takes four sliders to lift.

After strapping the diamond carefully onto the sledge and covering it with a tarp, you start the trip back the way you came. With the sledge being overloaded, it takes you twice the length of time to get back past the Tryon Cliffs and along the tracks to the top of Long Gully.

It takes a couple days to retrace your slide, but the closer you get to home, the more animated your troop becomes. Everyone is laughing and telling jokes. Some sing songs.

Dagma, knowing that more food is close to hand, has no hesitation in eating her last two energy bars.

Finally, after camping out for two more nights, the shimmering Pillars of Haramon appear in the distance. It is only then that you truly feel your mission has been a success.

Crew from the base are outside the loading bay when your sledges pull up. You can even see they've put a burner on for broth.

"How did it go?" one of the crew asks. "Find anything?"

"No nothing," Piver says trying to keep a straight face. "Except a great big red diamond! Geebus, you should see the size of it!"

Congratulations you've finished this part of the story. You've led a successful mission and found red diamonds that will help in your community's efforts to build the much needed trade routes between the Highlands and the Lowlands.

But have you followed all the different paths the story

takes?

It is time to make another decision. Do you:

Go to the start of the story and try another path? **P1**

Or

Go to the list of choices and start reading from another part of the story? **P204**

You have decided to go down and around the Tyron Cliffs.

You point at the contour marks on Gagnon's map. "I don't think the Lowlanders will be able to handle the steep terrain if we go up. I'm not even sure that we can. We'd better go down and around."

Gagnon nods. "Let's just hope everyone's legs hold out on the climb back up."

It is a risk, but what else can you do? You're convinced there will be accidents if you try to push a route up. Previous volcanic activity has left the upper slope littered with obstacles. And then there's the matter of the thin air. Less oxygen means tired muscles.

"Okay everyone," you say. "Three brakes in the back, one up front steering. And keep your speed down. These sledges are heavy. If they get away on you, you'll be going to the bottom and not in a good way."

Gagnon and Shoola move to the back of their respective sledges and organize the extra sliders. You and Gagnon, being the most experienced sliders, take control of the steering runners at attach yourselves to the front. Trodie and Piver free-slide while the others climb aboard the sledges.

You let Gagnon, the better navigator, lead off. "We'll keep the cliffs in sight," he says. "But be ready to stop in a hurry, this area isn't fully mapped and who knows what we'll find."

With that said, he leads off with a slight push of his stick. Gravity does the rest.

The screech of hooks is a constant companion as your group works its way down the mountain. Dagma, Shoola and the other sliders are working hard to keep the sledges from gaining too much momentum during the turns.

Gagnon takes a zigzag route. A quarter mile away from the cliffs and then a quarter mile back, keeping the sledges side on the slopes as much as possible.

You're just beginning to think the day is going to go by without incident when you hear a yell from the front sledge.

It's Gagnon, calling for an emergency stop.

"What is it?" you call. "Why are we stopping?"

"Take your light and shine it on the ground at your feet," he says.

"Why?"

"Just do it. You'll see what I mean."

Confused, you detach the headlamp from your helmet and point it towards the ground. As the bright light nears the surface, you see the beam penetrate the black glass and go right through to the other side. "What the—"

Then you realize what Gagnon's trying to say. You're not on solid ground at all. Your troop is traveling across a glass bridge suspended over a massive crevasse. Sure, black glass is tough stuff, but here it can't be more than a six inches thick.

"Holy moly," you say under your breath. "I wonder how deep the crevasse is."

"Stay where you are," Gagnon say. "Best if we move one at a time."

"What's going on?" Dagma asks

"We're sliding on a glassed-over crevasse," you say, trying to keep the fear out of your voice. "I don't suggest you stomp around at the moment, otherwise you might break through."

"Geebus," Piver says, having overheard. "I'm glad I'm not riding on a sledge."

You give Piver a sharp glance for scaring the Lowlanders. "The weight's spread evenly over the runners," you say. "Don't worry, everyone will be fine."

Or at least you hope they'll be fine.

With a wave you signal Gagnon to move out. "We'll stay here until you get on to solid rock. Signal us when you're clear."

The first sledge slides slowly downhill. Gagnon has his headlamp strapped to his right thigh so the light shines down on the ground in front of him. He slides another twenty yards before the glass no longer allows the light to penetrate and he screeches to a stop and waves his arm.

"Okay everyone, it's our turn. Slow and easy now," you say with a slight push. "No sudden movements."

Your shoulders tighten as the sledge slides towards

Gagnon. Faint tinking sounds vibrate through the ground as the crystalline structure of the glass fractures as the weighty sledge passes over it.

It isn't until you've reached Gagnon that you breathe easy. "I don't want to do that again in a hurry," you say. "That was way too freaky."

"Unfortunately, these bridges look just like the ground until you're on them," Gagnon says. "We can only cross our fingers and hope there aren't many more."

Then you have a thought. "Hey, Gagnon. I want you to disconnect and scout out front. We'll put Drexel on the front of your sledge."

Gagnon nods. "Good idea. If I see a glass bridge, we can head closer to the cliffs where the ground will be more solid."

As you look out over the landscape you see the Tyron Cliffs stretch off in the distance. Another day of this is going to test your nerve. The air is cool as you suck it into your lungs. You try to admire the beauty around you rather than think of the possible dangers. Worrying about something you can't change is pointless. You've been given a job and all you can do is your best. But before you have time to move out again. Piver breaks the silence.

"Hey," the little engineer says. "I've got an idea."

Please to hear any idea that might make your expedition a success, you look towards Piver. "Okay I'm listening."

"Well," Piver says. "This huge crevasse we've just slid over…"

"Yes?"

"I wonder how far it goes?"

You don't quite understand what Piver is trying to get at. "Why does that matter?"

"Well what if it cuts under the cliffs? What if we can break through the glass surface of the bridge and use the crevasse as a tunnel under the cliffs?"

You have a think for a moment. "Gagnon? What do you think?"

You can see that the navigator is thinking hard about Piver's theory. "It's worth checking out I suppose," Gagnon says.

You nod, "My thoughts exactly."

"Okay, Piver, let's do it. Just be careful, I don't want you falling in."

Piver giggles nervously. "You're not the only one."

Piver searches through the gear on the sledges and finds a bright chemical light and a couple of extra anchor-bolt guns. He puts in one anchor and hooks a line to his harness. Then he slowly walks back out looking for the edge of the crevasse.

About ten yards out, he stops. "Okay, this is where the solid rock ends. Time to find out how hard this glass really is."

You know that black glass is very strong in some ways, but not so strong in others. It can withstand huge pressure, but is not very shock resistant. Bridges have been known to hold a weighty sledge and then shatter when someone drops a cup of broth.

Piver points an anchor-bolt gun at the glassy surface, lowers his visor, and pulls the trigger. *Bang!* The anchor-bolt slams into the surface. At first nothing happens. Then you hear a faint tinkling sound and you know that a shock wave is running through the glass weakening it.

Bang! In goes the second bolt.

This time the ground at Piver's feet cracks into a thousand pieces and crashes down into the crevasse. Piver only just manages to jump back in time.

"Wow!" he cries. "Did you see that!"

You move a little closer and look through the gaping hole Piver's created. The crevasse is deep, but there is a narrow ledge running along its side about twenty feet down.

"Looks like a series of earthquakes have caused this," you say, looking down. "I wonder if this ledge runs all the way under the cliffs?"

"I could check it out," Piver says.

You admire Piver's courage. "Let's both check it out eh?" You turn towards the others. "Hey, Dagma, would you please get some cable and lower us down?"

As your feet touch the ledge a few minutes later,

you're pleased it slopes towards the wall and not the other way. At least you won't need to worry about slipping off into the void. You switch on your headlamp and push off. "Stay close, Piver."

As you and Piver slide along the narrow ledge, it doesn't take long before the light coming through the hole in the surface fades. The light from your headlamp begins to show up tiny specks of blue and red in the shiny black walls of the crevasse.

"It's like looking into the sky on a clear night," Piver says behind you.

The further you go, the bigger the flecks becomes. The scene is mesmerizing. You slide on in a semi-trance admiring the beauty before you.

"We must be under the cliffs," Piver says. "The added pressure has formed crystals."

Within another fifty yards, the wall has gone from having flecks to having wide veins of blue and red crystals.

"Wow, it's like another world down here," you say. "Like a dream."

"You do realize this wall is full of tyranium and diamonds don't you?" Piver says. "I'm not sure what the red is, but it looks like diamond with a faint trace of something else in it."

"Can we mine it?" you ask.

"Geebus yes! We've struck the jackpot."

The place you've discovered is so beautiful you don't want to leave. "I suppose we'd better get back and tell the others."

Piver sits on the ledge, his legs dangling over the edge. "Maybe we could just sit and enjoy it for a while?"

You sit down beside the little engineer and breathe a sigh of relief. "What a good idea, Piver. We'll never have the opportunity to see this for the first time again. We should enjoy the moment."

In a few minutes you'll let the other know what you've found, but for now you just want to take it all in.

"This has got to be the biggest find in history," Piver says. "We're gonna be famous. Our grandchildren will talk of this find."

"I suppose they will. I just hope it doesn't change us too much," you say. "I like my life at the moment. All I ever wanted to be was a member of the Highland Slider Corps."

Piver sneaks you a glance and grins. "Geebus, you'll always be one of those. Didn't they tell you when you signed up? It's a lifetime contract!"

Congratulations. This part of your story is over. You've lead a successful mission and found a rich source of tyranium and diamonds.

Your community will be very pleased. But have you tried all the paths? Have you been to the interior? Or the volcano?

It is time to make one of these three decisions. Do you.

Go back to the beginning and try another path? **P1**

Or

Go to the list of choices and start reading from another part of the story? **P204**

Or

Or go read some interesting things about the history of Petron? **P201**

You have decided to go check out the spaceship.

"Let go check it out," you say. "If they've come all this way to find us the least we can do is say hello."

Gagnon frowns. "But what if they're unfriendly?"

"If they're smart enough to build a craft that can travel though space, surely they must be smart enough to realize that fighting is just a waste of time and resources."

Gagnon doesn't seem convinced by your argument so you give him a choice, "Well I'm going to check them out. I'll leave it up to the rest of you if you want to join me."

The two of you slide back down to camp and explain to the others what you've found. Everybody but Villum is excited and wants to come along.

"Okay Villum, you stay here and guard the sledge. We'll see you in a while."

"Pango head," Piver mumbles under his breath. "What sort of idiot doesn't want to check out a space ship?"

As you slide towards the ship, more of its detail becomes visible. The outer covering is made from tiny metallic feathers of gold and silver. Ports in the ship's side have covers that open and close like the iris of your eyes.

"Geebus!" Piver says. "It's a beautiful piece of engineering."

When your group is twenty yards away. A port opens

and a set of steps swing out. A person, in uniform, walks out onto the top step and waves.

"Ahoy there!"

"Wow," you say. "They speak our language."

After sliding a little closer you see that the young person is a female about your age. Her long dark hair is braided and coiled on top of her head.

"Gre—Greetings." you say.

"Thanks," she says with a smile. "Are you the leader of this group?"

"Yes."

"Would you like to step aboard so we can talk? I mean you no harm."

You look over at Piver and then at Gagnon. Both are nodding their heads. The girl seems friendly. "Well um … okay."

She takes you to a small control room and offers you a seat. "This must be a shock for you."

"It is a bit. What brings you here?"

"My name is Helena. I'm commander of this landing pod from the *Victoria II* which is currently in orbit. Long ago, our ancestors discovered this planet while looking for a new home. On their travels between the stars, they sent three landing craft full of settlers and equipment down to this planet's surface in the hopes that they would establish colonies here and prosper."

You look at Helena. "You seem so young to be a

commander. How do you know how to fly this thing?"

"I'm not much younger than you. But to answer your question, while we sleep in our cryo-chambers, we learn all sorts of things, we just don't age much. I've been trained in communications, languages, navigation and I'm a fully qualified pilot. I've been woken up to come down and see how our cousins on Petron are doing."

"So we're related, your people and mine?" you ask, still trying to get your head around what the girl is saying.

"Yes. Distantly. The results of our survey show that descendants of all three groups have survived."

"Three groups?"

"Yes, three. The Highlanders, those you call Lowlanders and descendents of Eve, whose family settled in the jungle of the interior."

"There are people in the interior?"

"Yes, you've been heading in their direction for the last couple days. Once you reach the eastern end of this mountain range you will start finding their settlements."

Your head is spinning with all this new information. So the crazy miner who found tyranium in the interior has already met these people?" you ask.

"He was one of our scouts gathering information."

"Are these people in the interior dangerous?" you ask.

The girl laughs. "No not at all as long as you're honest with them. And they're keen to start trading now that the Highlanders and the Lowlanders have settled your differences and have called a truce. They have plenty of tyranium crystals to trade. They have advanced mining machines and other technology you Highlanders haven't developed yet. Trade will be good for all three settlements."

This news sounds great. "But what do they want in return?" you ask.

The girl smiles. "It seems our inland cousins have grown rather fond of roast pango. Something I believe you Highlanders have in great abundance."

You can't help but laugh. "Tyranium for pangos? Sounds like a good deal to me."

Helena stands and calls out some instructions to her crew. "Would you like to take a quick trip with me to set up a meeting? It will only take a few minutes to get to their settlement in our ship and will save you a few days slide."

"Fly in your machine? Really?"

"Sure, we have room for you and one other if you like."

You know exactly who to take along on the trip. From the top of the step you look down at the rest of your troop. "Gagnon, can you take charge for a few hours, I'm going to go find us some tyranium."

Gagnon nods.

"Piver, would you like to come for a ride?"

Piver's eyes pop with excitement. "Really? Me?"

"Yes you. Now hurry up and climb aboard."

The little engineer wastes no time getting up the steps. He caresses the hull of the ship as he enters through the portal. "Geebus!" Piver say. "This thing is amazing."

Piver's excitement is contagious. Soon both of you have wide grins on your faces.

"Okay, buckle up for takeoff," the young commander says pointing you to a couple of seats.

The door closes and you feel a low vibration run through the hull of the ship. Then, you feel the ship lift off.

"I'll leave the viewport open so you can see the sights," the young commander says.

Then, as if by magic, the craft streaks off around the last of the mountains before turning northwest towards a large lake in the distance.

"Oh, there's one thing I forgot to tell you. Although all Petronians have some plant DNA spliced into them so they can breathe the carbon dioxide rich atmosphere here on this planet, those of the interior are almost as much plant as they are human. So don't be surprised if they grow a tendril and wrap it around your hand. It's just their way of being friendly."

"Geebus!" Piver says, having the time of his life. "This should be interesting!"

Congratulations. This part of your story is over. You're

off to set up a meeting with the people of the interior to exchange pangos for the tyranium your communities need. You've also made contact with the *Victoria II* and learned some interesting facts about your planet's history.

But have you tried all the different paths this story can take? Have you been to Crater Canyon, or the volcano, Kakona? Have you fought off the morph rats or discovered giant crystals?

It is now time to make another decision. Do you:

Go back to the very beginning of the story and try another path? **P1**

Or

Go to the list of choices and start reading from another part of the story? **P204**

Or

Learn more about the planets history? **P201**

You have decided to observe the spaceship from a distance.

You look through your scope at the ship again. "I don't see any movement over there. Maybe whoever's in that thing hasn't seen us yet."

Gagnon instinctively crouches down as you continue to study the craft.

"So what do you think?" Gagnon asks. "Should we get the heck out of here?"

You shake your head. "No let's get back to the others and tell them to keep hidden. I want to hang around and find out what this thing is up to."

The troop is in the process of packing up when you and Gagnon slide back into camp. "Quiet everyone. There's been a development."

As you explain what you've seen, there are a variety of reactions. Dagma wants to slide right over to the ship and demand to know what they're doing on the Black Slopes. Piver wants to go over too, but so that he can study the craft from an engineering perspective.

A nervous Villum wants to slide home as fast as possible and then come back in force, while Trodie is interested in the newcomers but cautious.

You pull Trodie aside. "What we do now could have big consequences. Any suggestions?"

Trodie scratches the back of his neck as he thinks.

"This could be a good thing. I mean why would they come all this way just to hurt us? There are billions of planets out there. What are the chances of them finding ours unless they knew we were here to begin with?"

"You think they've been here before?"

Trodie shrugs. "It's possible. And isn't that what the *Book of Myths* says?"

"But those stories aren't real." And then you realize how silly what you just said was. "Or are they?"

"Maybe we should go check it out. Find out once and for all."

You are about to agree with Trodie when you feel a low vibration in your chest. When you look across the slope, you see that the disk is off the ground and a strange blue light is radiating from it. Once it's a hundred feet or so off the ground, the ship takes off like a bolt of lightning into the sky.

"Geebus, look at it go!" Piver says, twisting his neck so he can follow the ship's path.

Within seconds, all you can see is a blue speck high overhead.

"Look," Piver says, pointing upwards. "There's another one!"

A larger ship has come over the horizon and is heading towards the disk that has just taken off.

"It's going back to the mother ship." Trodie says. "That's written about in the book too."

"*... and children of the mother ship were sent to seed the planet,*" you quote from the *Book of Myths*, remembering the stories you've read ever since you were a child.

Trodie shrugs. "I'm not normally one to believe in fairytales, but I'm willing to change my mind when presented with solid evidence."

"So do we carry on in our mission, or do we go back and report this?" Gagnon says.

"I want to see the spot where it landed," Piver pipes up. "They could have left something behind."

What Piver says makes sense.

"Okay, let's go check it out," you say. "The rest of you, finish the loading and get ready to move out."

It's a quick slide to the spot where the ship was standing and at first, apart from a few scorch marks and some strange dust, the black rock looks the same as everywhere else. But as you are about to suggest a return to the troop, Piver notices a small yellow disk imbedded in the slope.

"What is it?" you ask.

Piver pulls a probe out of his utility belt. He gets onto his knees and wedges it under the edge of the disk.

"It won't budge," the little engineer says. "I think it's fused into the rock." Piver raps the disk a few times with the probe's handle and then stands. "It sounds hollow."

A faint tremor runs though the rock beneath your feet.

"Geebus! Do you feel that? The ground's vibrating."

You point at the disk in the rock. "Is that thing causing it?"

Then with a crackling buzz a beam of light, brighter than the strongest torch, shoots out of the disk and up towards the stratosphere.

"What's going on?" you ask Piver. "And why would they leave a light?"

Piver looks nervous. He looks up in the sky, back at the disk, then back at the sky again. His hands are shaking. He knows something that he's not telling you.

"What is it, Piver?"

"I think it's a landing beacon."

"But the only reason they'd need a landing beacon is if they were—."

"Coming back!"

This news is a shock. What do you do? It is time to make a decision. Do you:

Wait for the ship to return? **P186**

Or

Go back to the Pillars and report the ship? **P194**

You have decided to wait for the ship to return.

Suddenly the light goes off.

"I must have triggered it somehow," Piver says. "What should we do?"

"I think we should wait for the ship to return," you say. "We need to find out what they are up to and if our communities are in danger."

Piver agrees. The two of you slide back over to your troop. When you tell them your plan, most of the sliders nod their heads in agreement. But you see doubt in Gagnon's face.

"What's the matter, Gagnon? You disagree?"

"But how do we know how long they will be?" he says. "It could take years for them to return."

You look up. The mother ship is still visible near the horizon. "Okay, you've got a point. If they don't come back by tomorrow morning, we'll go back to the Pillars and make a report. In the meantime let's move closer to the landing zone. I want a better look at them if they come back down."

Gagnon has his scope out and has spotted a fissure in the slope just above the landing spot. He points towards it. "We can hide in that crack while we wait."

"Good idea, Gagnon," Dagma says. "That way we'll be above them if we need to attack."

You spin and face Dagma. "Take it easy, who said

anything about attacking?"

"But…"

"If this ship has come across the galaxy, do you really think its occupants would have any problem dealing with half a dozen sliders with guide sticks and catapults?"

Dagma kicks the ground with her boot. "But I…"

You give the big slider a friendly smile. "Look, I know you meant well. Now, put on your happy face and let's climb up and get settled in that crevasse."

With that, your troop gets ready to move off. The spot Gagnon's located is about 200 yards above the landing beacon.

Once you're all hunkered down, a black tarp, normally used to cover the sledge, is rigged up to hide your position from above. Dagma lights a burner and gets some broth heating.

"We'll take turns on watch," you tell your troop. "An hour each."

As the others nap and tell stories, a lookout watches the ship for signs of activity. An hour later Shoola shouts a warning.

"It's moving west!" she yells

Everyone leaps to their feet and watches as the mother ship moves slowly westward, towards the Pillars of Haramon and disappears beyond the horizon.

"What are they doing?" Piver asks. "Are they going to attack the Pillars?"

"I don't know," you say. "But we can't hang around here any longer. Get loaded everyone. We're sliding top speed to the Pillars."

"Geebus, top speed?"

You nod. "That's right. We'll leave the sledge here and take only what we can carry."

Trodie is concerned. "I don't think Villum and I can slide as quickly as you Highlanders."

Trodie's right of course. They are Lowlanders after all.

"Okay, Drexel can stay with you two. Just slide at a pace that keeps you safe. The rest of us are going to go for it. The Pillars might need all the help they can get."

Sliders are well trained to pack and move quickly. In less than five minutes you, Gagnon, Dagma, Piver and Shoola are ready to move out. Drexel looks a little anxious. He's not that keen about being left behind with Trodie and Villum but he also knows why you've done it and will carry out his instructions to the best of his ability.

"Okay, Sliders on my mark!"

And away you slide, crouching low, your arms tucked to your side to reduce drag, with toes pointed downhill just that little bit more, letting gravity speed you across the slope.

The first run is done in ultra-quick time. When you've lost all the altitude you can afford, Piver sets up a portable launcher and fires a bolt into a pinnacle up the

slope. You clamp on your zipper and let it pull you up
the fine cable. After removing the bolt, Piver repeats the
process until your group has regained enough altitude to
start another high-speed traverse.

The speed is exciting. You love traversing as fast as
you can. It's a skill you've learned well. But after sliding
most of the day your leg muscles burn and sweat drips
down your back. Because of the speed you're traveling at,
you've nearly fallen a few times. Thankfully a quick tap
with your guide stick stops you from plummeting to the
bottom.

Dagma urges everyone on. Her endurance is only
exceeded by her need for competition. The slide to the
Pillars soon turns into a race, with each slider determined
to be first to the next waypoint.

Piver slides well. His low centre of gravity keeps him
balanced. And he's smart. At one point you see him hook
onto Dagma's backpack without her realizing it and get a
free ride in her slipstream. When she screeches into the
waypoint ready for the next zip uphill, her jaw nearly hits
the ground when she turns around and discovers Piver
standing there giggling with barely a drop of sweat on his
brow.

The sun is low and it's nearly dewfall before you see
the Pillars of Haramon. Your muscles ache and you back
is stiff from the headlong slide back to Long Gully.

You take out your scope and scan the terrain below,

not wanting to slide into a trap should the strange flying craft be in control of the base. It isn't until your lens moves up towards the command pod on the northernmost pillar that you see the silver disk sitting on top of the tower.

Gagnon has his scope trained on the pillars too.

"Do you see what I see, Gagnon?" you ask.

"I don't see any fighting going on," he replies. "Everything looks normal."

The navigator is right. You can see sliders going about their normal business. Being near dewfall, sledges are being move into their storage pods and the cableway between the two pillars is moving workers from the command pillar to the accommodation pods in the smaller pillar further down Long Gully.

"It's getting late. Let's go," you say, pointing you foot downhill and pushing off with your stick.

Piver rockets past you. "Last one home's a pango's bum!"

And with that the race is back on. Dagma pushes hard with her stick and drops into a slider's crouch. Her extra weight gives her an advantage over the much lighter Piver. But Piver cuts a clean turn and it isn't easy for Dagma to catch him until he is nearly outside the command pillar. She reaches out with her guide stick and hooks Piver's backpack, pulling the little engineer back.

"That's not fair!" Piver yells as they screech to a halt

on the loading platform. "You hooked me!"

The two are still arguing when you and the others slide up. "Piver! Just let it go."

Piver gives you a smile. "Geebus okay. Don't get your boots in a tangle."

"Besides," you say. "I seem to recall you doing something similar not that long ago?"

Piver giggles and turns to Dagma. "Good race. Let's call it a tie."

With your troop happy again, you waste no time entering the pillar and jumping a cable lift up to the command pod. When you step off the lift, members of the council are sitting around the table talking to a young woman dressed in a uniform you don't recognize.

"Ah," the chief says when he sees you. "Come … join us. You look like you've had a long slide." As you walk towards the table, the chief stands. "Let me introduce you to our guest."

"Hello," you say, bumping elbows with the visitor. "We saw you further east and decided to—"

"Make sure we weren't attacking your outpost?" the visitor says.

You can feel your face redden.

"Don't worry. I would have done the same," she says.

"Sit," the chief says. "We've been learning lots of interesting things this afternoon. Commander Helena is from a planet in another solar system. Seems we're related."

"Really?" you say.

"Distantly," the young commander says. "Our ancestors settled this planet many generations ago while traveling between the stars to their new home."

The chief smiles. "She's come back to do a survey to see how we're doing."

You're not quite sure what to say. You've often wondered, while sliding around the Black Slopes, how life began on Petron and why you were here. But you never thought it was a question you'd get the answer to.

"Seems we have more relatives in the interior. Relatives with more tyranium than they know what to do with. Helena's offered to take us to them to talk trade."

'Wow," you say. "We're going to go of course?"

The chief stands. "That's what I want to speak to you about."

You cross your fingers and hope the chief is going to say what you think he is.

"I'd like you to go meet these people of the interior as our representative. You young people are the future of this planet. I think it's only right that you learn as much as possible from our guests in the short time they are here."

You find yourself smiling and nodding eagerly at the chief's suggestion.

"And," he says, "you're young enough, so that in 80

years time, you will still remember this day and be able to say to the others that you saw Helena's ship with your own eyes."

The visitor rests her hand on your shoulder. "I have room in my ship for you to bring a friend along if you'd like. We'll leave first thing tomorrow morning."

"Now I'm sure you're tired after your slide," the chief says. "Go get some rest at report here at sunrise."

You head back down to where your troop is drinking broth and chatting in one of the storage bays. After explaining what you've discovered you have one last piece of news to impart.

"Hey Piver, the commander of the landing ship says I can take a friend along tomorrow when we go to visit the interior. Would you like to come?"

Piver's eye widen, his hands clasp in front of his chest and he does a little jiggle as he looks up at you. "You mean fly in the ship? Geebus! Would I ever!"

Congratulations, this part of your story is over. But have you tried all the different paths this story can take? Have you been to Crater Canyon, or the volcano?

It is time to make a decision. Do you:

Go to the beginning and read a different path? **P1**

Or

Go to the list of choices and pick another place to start? **P204**

You have decided to go back to the Pillars and report the ship.

"We need to let Command know about this," you say.

You and Piver race back to your troop.

"Dagma, Shoola, Gagnon, get loaded. We're sliding top speed to the Pillars."

"Geebus, top speed?" Piver says.

You nod. "That's right. We'll leave the sledge here and take only what we can carry."

Trodie seems concerned. "What about us? You can't just leave us here."

Trodie's right of course. They are Lowlanders after all.

"Drexel, I need you to escort the Lowlanders back to the Pillars. Just slide at a pace that keeps them safe."

Drexel doesn't look happy, but you know he'll follow orders.

It takes less than five minutes before you and your reduced troop are ready to move out.

"Okay, on my mark! Sticks tight and knees bent."

Piver locks his boots together, ready for the high-speed slide. "Geebus! This should be interesting."

And away you slide, with feet pointed downhill just that little bit more, letting gravity speed you across the slippery black rock.

Despite the urgency of your slide and the wind whistling past your visor, you still have a chance to sneak a glance at the view from time to time. This is the part of being a slider that you love most. Far below, the high meadows are covered in green. Beyond the meadows patterned fields of the Lowland crops stretch all the way to the sea. It is a view you never tire of.

The first run of eight miles is done in record time.

"Set up a launcher and lets gain some more altitude, Piver."

The engineer works quickly. He fires a bolt into a pinnacle further up the slope and everyone clamps on and lets their zippers pull them up the fine cable. After removing the bolt, Piver repeats the process until your group has regained enough altitude to start sliding again.

Dagma races past you. "Come on, we're never going to get home if you slide like my grandmother."

Shoola crouches down lower and pushes hard with her stick in an effort to keep up with her arch rival.

Neither of them see the patch of morph rat slime in their path until it's too late.

Dagma hits the patch of slippery goo and immediately loses her feet. Without the grip her glide boots provide, she immediately veers off down the mountain.

Shoola has enough time to drop her hooks, but she still hits the slime at speed and falls.

Thankfully you and the others are fifty yards back. "Stop!" you yell, dropping your hook just in time to avoid the stinky mess.

You hear the screech of hooks on the mountain below you. Dagma and Shoola are both putting their full weight on their hooks in an attempt to stop.

From your position, you watch the drama unfold. Further down the hill is a pinnacle. Maybe Dagma or Shoola will be able to get an anchor into that. It may be their only chance.

You pull out your scope to follow the action. Dagma has her anchor gun out. "Come on Dagma! You can do it!" you yell in encouragement.

Dagma licks her lips and pulls the trigger. The bolt shoots out of her anchor gun and hits the pinnacle. Now it just needs to hold.

As the cable tightens, Dagma's line down the mountain is altered and she begins to swing in the direction of pinnacle.

Then you see Shoola pull out her anchor gun. But the pinnacle is too far away for her to hit it. None the less she is taking aim at something.

With a pop, Shoola's anchor bolt rockets towards Dagma.

"Ouch!" Dagma yells. "You shot me in the bum!"

Dagma stabs a glance at Shoola then grabs the fine line protruding from her buttock, and wraps it around her wrist so the anchor doesn't pull out and Shoola doesn't fall.. "Just you wait Shoola!"

"They're stopping!" you tell the others. "Dagma's line

is holding."

Piver is already moving. He has a portable winch set up and is lowering a line to the two sliders.

It takes about half an hour to winch Dagma and Shoola back up to safety. Dagma is limping and in pain from the wound in her backside. Shoola supports her. Once they are both out of danger, Gagnon puts a medical dressing on Dagma's injury and gives her a squirt of moth mist to deaden the pain.

"You owe me, Shoola," Dagma says.

Shoola laughs, "Just as well I had a big target to aim at, otherwise I'd be heading for the bottom."

Then she pulls out a couple energy bars and hands them to Dagma. "Here eat these, that'll take your mind off things."

"Okay everyone, we need to get moving," you say. "Can you slide Dagma?"

Dagma nods. "As long as that pango headed Shoola doesn't shoot in the bum again I'll be fine."

"Right then. Let's get around this patch of slime and get moving."

After another two hour's sliding, your leg muscles ache and your forehead is covered in sweat. It is nearly dewfall before you see the Pillars of Haramon.

You take out your scope and scan the terrain below. "Looks peaceful enough."

Gagnon has his scope out too. "The ship is on top of

the command pillar, but I don't see any panic."

The navigator is right. Sliders going about their normal business.

"It must be okay. Dewfall's not far away. Let's go," you say as you point you toe downhill.

Once you arrive, you waste no time jumping a cable lift up to the command pod. When you step off the lift, you see that the council is sitting around the table talking to a young woman dressed in uniform. The Lowland general is here too.

"Ah," the chief says when he sees you. "Come … join us. You look like you've had a long day." As you walk towards the table, the chief stands. "Let me introduce you to our guest. This is Helena, commander of the landing craft and representative of Earth II."

You smile at the visitor.

"Sit," the chief says, pulling out a chair. "We've been learning lots of interesting things this afternoon. Our guest here is from a planet in a nearby solar system. Seems we're related."

"Really?" you say.

"Distantly," the young woman says. "Our ancestors settled this planet long ago while traveling between the stars to their new home."

You're not quite sure what to say. It's all a bit of a shock.

"Seems we have more relatives in the interior," the

chief says. "Relatives with more tyranium than they know what to do with."

'Wow," you say. "Are they friendly?"

Helena smiles. "As long are you are honest with them, you'll have no problems. But that isn't the reason I'm here."

The chief stands and comes around to where you are sitting. "Now that's what I want to speak to you about." The chief pats you on the shoulder. "I'd like you to go with Helena and be our ambassador to their planet. The time has come to start trading. We have minerals on this planet they need. And they have technology we need. It will be very beneficial for us both. Young people are the future of both planets. That's why I think it's only right that you become our representative ."

You find yourself smiling at the chief's suggestion. What an adventure it will be.

Helena comes to stand beside you. "I have room in my ship for you to bring a friend along if you'd like."

After Helena has answered all your questions, you head back down to where your troop is drinking broth and chatting in one of the storage bays. You can't quite believe how excited you are. After explaining what you've discovered you have one last piece of news to impart.

"Hey, Piver. The commander of the landing ship says I can take a friend along. Are you interested in a trip between the stars?"

Piver's eyes widen and his hands clasp in front of his chest as he looks up at you. "You mean all the way to another planet, in their spaceship?" Piver does a funny little jiggle. "Geebus! Would I ever!"

Congratulations, this part of your story is over. But have you tried all the different paths this story can take? Have you been to Crater Canyon, or to the volcano? Have you fought off the morph rats or discovered giant crystals?

It is time to make a decision. Do you:

Go back to the very beginning of the story and take a different path? **P1**

Or

Go to the list of choices and start reading from another part of the story? **P204**

History of Petron.

The Black Slopes are the mountainous region of Petron, the fourth planet circling a yellow-dwarf sun 12,000 light years from the centre of a galaxy, known by some as Andromeda.

The Black Slopes are made from volcanic glass that erupted from Petron's core not long after its formation some 13 billion years ago. As it cooled and hardened, this magma formed razor sharp ridges, half pipes, steep valleys, near vertical cliffs and towering pinnacles. It is a landscape that is beautiful and dangerous.

Petron was colonized long, long ago, by people from another galaxy.

There are three groups living on Petron. The Lowlanders, who farm and fish, the Highlanders who live high on the Black Slopes, and the Others on the far side of the mountains. The Others are the descendents of Eva and her family. Some of this family are part plant and animal. You'll meet them, as well as space pirates, game playing monkeys, and other characters if you read BETWEEN THE STARS.

You are a Highlander, of that you and your family are very proud.

The Highland Sliders are not only a defense force, they are also expert guides, equipped to escort others along a system of tracks the Highlanders have constructed between the various communities, hydro growing centers, and mining operations over the generations. Without a highly trained Slider escort, traveling around the slopes would be near impossible.

But even highly trained Sliders with their tyranium needle-crystal boots and diamond tipped guide sticks know to watch their step on the Black Slopes when it rains.

Although currently at peace, the Lowlanders and Highlanders of Petron haven't always been friendly. For many generations the Lowlanders tried to conquer the Highlands so they could gain access to the Highland's rich mineral deposits and the huge colonies of red-beaked pangos, a bird that provides one of the planet's most valuable and tasty sources of protein. For generations the Highland Slider Corps repelled these invasions. You can read about this conflict in the book SECRETS OF GLASS MOUNTAIN.

It is time to make a decision. Do you:

Go back to the very beginning of the story and try another path? **P1**

Or

Go to the list of choices and read from another part of the story? **P204**

More 'you say which way' adventures.

Pirate Island

Between the Stars

Lost in Lion Country

Once Upon an Island

In the Magician's House

Secrets of Glass Mountain

Danger on Dolphin Island

The Sorcerer's Maze - Jungle Trek

The Sorcerer's Maze - Adventure Quiz

List of Choices

Made in the USA
Middletown, DE
20 February 2018